Dawson: When he meets lovely foreigner Sheila, he's inspired to film a whole new story. But somehow real life just won't follow the script.

Joey: Slender and dark-haired, she's annoyed that Dawson's met someone new. After all, *she's* supposed to be Dawson's best friend. Then gorgeous volleyball player Jeremy shows up at the beach. . . .

Pacey: He joins the summer lifeguard class to meet hot girls. But he ends up saving a life.

Jen: Pacey's really getting on her nerves. But she's not about to let him distract her from her CPR training. Good thing—because she's going to need it very soon.

DAWSON'S CREEK™

Dawson's Creek™

Long Hot Summer

Based on the television series "Dawson's Creek™"
created by **Kevin Williamson**

Written by **K. S. Rodriguez**

CHANNEL 4 BOOKS

First published 1998 by Pocket Books, a division of
Simon and Schuster Inc., New York

First published in Great Britain 1999 by Channel 4 Books
an imprint of Macmillan Publishers Ltd
25 Eccleston Place, London SW1W 9NF
Basingstoke and Oxford

Associated companies throughout the world

ISBN 0 7522 1372 5

11 13 15 17 19 18 16 14 12 10

A CIP catalogue record for this book is available from
the British Library.

Printed and bound in Great Britain by
Mackays of Chatham plc, Chatham, Kent

For Arthur Termott and Alexandra Peredo,
my favorite teenagers.

Chapter 1

*T*he girl races toward the dock, her expression turning from anguish to fear. A dead end. How would she escape? The hit man's urgent footsteps are pounding behind her, growing louder, coming closer and closer. . . .

She is the only living witness. The pretty, innocent teenager could blow the Capeside Connection wide open. If she doesn't get away and get help—fast—the mob will rub her out.

There is only one avenue of escape. Quickly she unties the rowboat attached to the dock. She scans the area—no other boats around. Perfect. If she can just find the oars, she'll be out of harm's way.

She spies the oars lying on the grass at the far end of the dock. But the hit man is in view now. He wears a wide-brimmed hat, pulled low over his dark and deadly eyes.

1

The girl anxiously looks from the oars to the hit man. He stretches an arm out and fires his first shot. Pow! She has no choice. She rushes to the paddles, risking her life with every second of delay.

Pow! Pow! She dodges the bullets. Luckily, the hit man misses, and she retrieves the oars. Tucking them under her arm, she races back down the dock, her long brown hair flying in the breeze.

Thump! She lands in the center of the rowboat. It wobbles and wavers, but the girl takes immediate control.

Pow! Plop! Pow! Plop! Gunshots sound, and bullets drop into the water around her. The girl doesn't hesitate. She doesn't flinch, and she doesn't look back. Dipping the oars into the water, she steadies the boat and glides quickly to a safe distance, taunting the hit man: "Does the Godfather know you're such a bad shot?"

The gunman throws down his weapon and curses in disgust. The girl, wearing a satisfied smile, continues to row. She knew joining the crew team would come in handy one day. Next year, she muses, maybe the skeet squad. "Target practice," she hollers triumphantly. "Look it up!"

"And it's a wrap!" Dawson Leery called out, still peering through the camera viewfinder at Joey Potter in the rowboat. He took a step closer to Joey as he faded out. "That was grea—"

Before he could finish his sentence, Dawson teetered off the end of the dock and plunked into the creek with a huge splash.

He surfaced and dunked his head backward into

the water so his hair slicked back like that of an old-time movie star. Hysterical laughter rang out around him. He saw Pacey Witter standing at the end of the dock, twirling the prop pistol. Joey still sat in the rowboat in the creek, a few feet away from Dawson.

"Smooth move, Baryshnikov," Pacey shouted.

Joey abruptly stopped laughing. "Hey!" she yelled from the boat. "Does this mean that all of that footage is ruined and we have to shoot this again?"

Dawson swam to the dock and handed Pacey the camera. "Nope—it's waterproof. I'm happy to say that *The Capeside Connection* is in the can."

Pacey whooped in celebration. He shed his hitman hat and overcoat, and cannonballed over Dawson's head into the creek.

"Now summer is really here!" Joey said happily.

Dawson looked toward her. She looked so nice and happy and dry in that rowboat. . . .

He locked eyes with Pacey. The good thing about having a friend like Pacey, Dawson thought, was that he always seemed to know exactly what Dawson was thinking. The second good thing was that he had the sickest and most mischievous sense of humor of anyone Dawson had ever met.

Dawson and Pacey swam over to the rowboat as Joey chattered on. "Can we lay off the filming for a while, now?" she was saying. "You've been working us like mules all year long, Dawson. I mean, I think your movies are good and everything, but they *are* a lot of work."

"Then stop complaining and join a union," Dawson said as he placed his hands on one side of the boat, while Pacey grabbed on to the other. They exchanged a roguish glance, but this time it didn't escape Joey.

She picked up an oar and poked it at Dawson as he playfully started to rock the boat. "Don't!" she cried. "Please—I don't want to get wet again! I'm finally dry from the last take! And I have to go to work," she pleaded.

Dawson stopped rocking the boat and gave Joey his best sincere stare. "Okay," he said, "if you say so."

The two boys suddenly gave the rowboat a mighty shove.

The boat tipped.

Joey screamed.

Into the creek she went.

This time Dawson got to laugh with Pacey at Joey.

"They're two exhibits short in the immaturity museum," Joey sputtered when she emerged. "You guys should really get over there."

Pacey gave Joey a splash. "But we took the day off for your induction into the premenstrual hall of fame," he retorted. "We wouldn't miss that for the world."

Dawson laughed so hard he nearly swallowed a mouthful of water. He spit it out, straight at Joey.

"This is war," Joey declared, then splashed both boys with all of her might.

Dawson and Pacey retaliated, while Joey sank into the water to escape the attack.

A familiar voice called them from the end of the dock.

"I thought you guys were going to finish that film today. No one told me anything about having fun!"

Dawson grinned. It was Jen Lindley. Though she was making an all-out effort to be friends again after their breakup, Dawson still felt a small pang in his heart that their romance had died.

Joey popped her head out of the water and regarded Jen's pale arm moving in a friendly wave. "Captain Ahab arrives" she murmured, then felt guilty. Somehow she just couldn't seem to stop herself from making comments about Jen, even though they were friends now, after a rocky start. Joey always felt so gawky around cool, sophisticated Jen.

Dawson shot Joey a look and splashed her in the face. Even though he told himself he was totally over Jen, he still didn't like it when Joey gave her a hard time. He still felt protective of Jen.

He admired how the sun glistened off Jen's golden hair as she dangled a delicate foot off the dock. His breath caught in his throat again. He thought she was so beautiful. Every time he saw her he felt something between wanting her to disappear and wanting her back.

Jen smiled. "How'd it go today, Dawson?" she asked, her voice amiable.

Dawson called back, "Great, great!" trying to sound casual.

But he didn't feel casual. Trying to be all buddy-buddy with Jen was hard. Harder than he had ever imagined.

Pacey's voice cut through Dawson's thoughts and lightened his mood. "Hey, Jen, if you want to join us, you have to take off your clothes," he joked, grabbing the overturned rowboat as Joey and Dawson treaded water. "You can't see, but we're all skinny-dipping."

Jen laughed and made circles in the water with her foot. "Nice try, Pacey. I think I'll keep my clothes on and stay dry."

Pacey didn't give up. "If you want to stay dry, you can sunbathe naked. Nude sunbathing is legal in Capeside, you know. It was one of America's first settled nudist colonies. Townspeople here pay homage to the nude settlers every summer by shedding their clothing at the drop of a hat."

"I'll pass on that, too, but thanks for the history lesson," she answered.

Joey mumbled, "That's funny. Nothing's ever stopped her from taking off her clothes before."

"Oooh—meow," Pacey said.

Dawson put a giant hand on top of Joey's head and dunked her for that comment. Joey was his closest friend—even closer than Pacey—but sometimes she could really tick him off.

Dawson sighed. He had so many conflicting feelings about Joey. Sometimes he wanted to strangle her. Other times he wanted to kiss her. It was weird. Weirder, if possible, than his relationship with Jen.

He thought about a time recently when he and Joey had kissed. It was strange, but since then he had started to think about her in a different way. In a—dared he say it?—sexual way. It was hard for him to reconcile the images of Joey, the girl who used to hide in his closet and play Jaws with him, and Joey, the girl with pretty, thick brown hair and incredibly soft lips. He tried to push both images out of his mind.

Joey came up sputtering from his dunk. "What's your problem, Dawson?" she sputtered, clearly annoyed.

Dawson didn't answer. He didn't know *what* his problem was.

Chapter 2

Dawson, Joey, Pacey, and Jen spent the rest of the afternoon lying on the dock. The warm summer sun soaking into Joey's skin felt great. She was so relaxed she almost felt as if she were floating. She wished she didn't have to go to work. She could lie on the dock for days, free from all responsibility, her body limp.

The foursome was mostly silent, listening to the cry of the gulls that circled overhead and enjoying the breeze that made the waves splash against the rocking rowboat.

Joey noted that Dawson was quiet. His mood had changed as soon as Jen arrived. That was typical, she thought. He'd been acting like some kind of psychology experiment lately. One minute he'd be fun. The next minute he'd act warm and fuzzy and thoughtful. Then in a flash he'd turn into a tortured, scowling, grunting, typical teenage male.

What had happened to the old Dawson? Joey wondered. She wished he would be his old self again—the guy who could finish her sentences or say what she was thinking before she even said it. She hoped they could actually have some fun this summer—if it was possible in between baby-sitting and working like a slave.

Work. "What time is it?" Joey asked, breaking the silence. She figured she'd have to get over to the Icehouse soon.

"Why?" Pacey asked lazily. "There was a big zoo break and you have a date?"

"No," Joey answered. "Unlike you three layabouts I have to go to work. So what time *is* it?"

"It's four o'clock," Dawson said, "and you forget the many grueling hours Pacey and I have ahead of us at Screenplay Video this summer."

"The many grueling hours *you* have ahead of you at Screenplay Video, my friend," Pacey spoke up. "I officially resigned yesterday."

Dawson sat upright. "What?" he asked incredulously. "Why did you quit?"

Pacey opened his eyes and shielded them from the late afternoon sun. "Because I have bigger and better opportunities."

"Like what?" Dawson scoffed. "Cleaning your dad's guns? Helping your mom garden? Watching the creek evaporate?"

"Opportunities like meeting women in bikinis," Pacey answered, slipping on his sunglasses. "Saving damsels in distress from shark attacks. Sitting in the sun all day and flexing my muscles—that kind of stuff. Like that Blotto song from the eighties, I wanna be a lifeguard. And I'm going to be a lifeguard. You heard it here first."

Jen laughed and uncrossed her legs from their yoga position.

"You think that's funny?" Pacey asked defensively, lowering his shades. He did his best mobster impersonation. "Do I amuse you?"

Jen shook her head. "No, of course not. It's just that—that's what I'm doing this summer, too. Are you going to start Lifesaving 101 at the town pool bright and early tomorrow?"

"Seven-thirty," Pacey confirmed. "Cool. I'm glad I'll know someone else there."

Jen smiled. "Yeah. Me too."

Joey smiled too. It was good to know that Jen would be busy this summer. Maybe then she'd stop hanging around and force-feeding her friendliness to everyone. That gave Joey an idea.

She stood up to leave, but she lingered for a moment. "Hey, Dawson," she said, jabbing him with her foot, "before these two start playing *Baywatch*, why don't we hit the beach while it's still safe? How about Friday? Early, though, because I have to work the late lunch shift."

Dawson seemed to come out of whatever dream world he was in and answered Joey with a startled and uncertain "Sure." Then he added, "I mean—sounds great. I'll pick you up."

"Don't forget the Frisbee," Joey added. "Bye, guys!" She jumped into her rowboat, grabbed the oars, and glided toward home, feeling warm inside, as if the heat from the sun were radiating through her chest.

She watched the three figures grow smaller with each pull of the oars. She decided right then and there that she was going to have a good summer if it killed her. Despite everything she had to do, she was determined to have fun and spend a lot of time with Dawson, like the old days.

Maybe then his head would come down from planet Jen and come back to Capeside.

And maybe he would even be her best friend again.

Chapter 3

"The sights and sounds of Capeside at night," Dawson said in his best narrative voice. Though he didn't know what he'd do with this tape, Dawson enjoyed filming bits and pieces of his favorite places.

Dawson zoomed in and out on the reflection of moonlight on the water. He stopped the tape and lowered his camera, then walked over and sat beneath the tall oak tree. He stretched out and took in a deep breath of the warm night air.

He loved to sit by the creek at night. It was all so quiet and still. This was the only place and evening was the only time when he could truly be alone with his thoughts. The events of the day played in his mind like a movie.

It was going to be weird working at the video store without Pacey. They were sure to be short-handed now, but it never was busy in the summer anyway. Who would he talk to all day?

He'd spend the day at the beach with Joey on Friday, as he had promised. But after that, he'd cool off until he got his feelings sorted out. Or until he met someone else.

But how and where would he meet someone new? Capeside was so small, and unfortunately most of the girls didn't hold his interest. He had to find something else to do this summer—something that would keep him busy, out of trouble, and away from girls whose names began with *J*.

Male-female relationships were just too complicated, Dawson thought. He never had to go through any of that with Pacey. It was like that movie, *When Harry Met Sally*. In that movie, Harry says that men and women can't be friends because "the sex part always gets in the way." Too true, Dawson thought.

Dawson lifted his camera and restarted the tape. He panned the shoreline across the way. Orange lights twinkled like out-of-focus fireflies in the distance. A cricket perched on a nearby bush chirped a high-pitched chant. Boats rocked softly on the dark water.

Then it hit him: he could make a documentary. He'd never tried that before. But a documentary about what? Capeside?

He had lived in Capeside all his life, and though he thought it was a pretty ordinary place, he loved many things about it. He especially liked it in the fall, when the tourists went home, the beaches grew quiet, and it returned to being a low-key seaside town. But as much as he liked the quaint town, he didn't think it would make for a very interesting documentary.

Dawson groaned. He could make a documentary about his own sorrowful life. It would be called *Dawson Leery: Inside Every Loser Is an Even Bigger Dork.* "You're pathetic," he said to himself.

He hoped a better idea would come to him eventually. As a cloud passed over the moon and the cricket's chirps grew louder, Dawson stole a sideways glance at his wristwatch: nine o'clock.

He aimed the camera toward the houses along the shore, deciding to speculate on what other people were up to at that time of night.

Next to Jen's house was the Backmans' place. They were probably having a family fight, Dawson guessed. Sometimes they screamed so loud at one another that people on the other side of the creek claimed they could hear them.

Next to the Backmans were the Barclays. He focused on their gray Cape Cod home. They were a nice young yuppie couple. Dawson's mother had told him they'd just had twins. They were probably holding hands by the cribside, watching the babies sleep peacefully.

He zoomed in closer when he saw a figure come out the back door of the Barclay's house. Dawson stood up. It was a young woman. He'd never seen *her* before.

She leaned against the wooden porch railing and stared across the creek. Dawson could see that she was beautiful. She looked about his age, but it was hard to tell from that distance.

"This calls for some investigation, Geraldo," Dawson said softly to himself.

Quietly he crept along the grass, careful not to let the girl see him. He stopped when he had a full-face close-up of her.

The camera didn't lie. She *was* beautiful. Seventeen, eighteen, nineteen, maybe, Dawson thought. Intrigued, he raised his eyebrows. An older woman. Cool.

The moonlight danced down the girl's long sandy-colored hair—the longest hair Dawson had ever seen, even longer than Joey's. Her profile was soft and fragile, her expression dreamy.

Who was this mysterious new girl? "Enquiring minds want to know," Dawson whispered.

The girl turned back toward the house, as if someone had called her inside. She walked quickly across the porch and disappeared. Dawson could hear the screen door shut.

Dawson stopped the tape. "Cut," he said thoughtfully.

He lowered the camera and jogged back to his own yard, a big grin on his face. Well, well, a new girl in town. Tomorrow he'd make it his business to find out who she was.

Chapter 4

Jen regarded herself in the full-length mirror in her bedroom. The new hot pink bikini fit perfectly, but she wasn't sure she should wear it on the first day of lifesaving class. Maybe she should wear a one-piece—something more modest.

A soft tap at her door interrupted her decision. "Come in, Grams," she said.

Jen's grandmother quietly opened the door and poked her head in. "Don't forget to wear sunblock," she said. Then her eyes widened when she noticed what her granddaughter was wearing. "Certainly you're not going to class in *that*," she said sternly.

That made up Jen's mind. Forget the one-piece. The hot pink bikini it was. Though she knew what Grams' beef was, Jen feigned ignorance. "What's wrong with this suit, Grams? Does it reveal that I am a young woman?" She put on an expression of mock horror. "Do you think people are going to notice my *breasts*?" she whispered in a fake shocked tone.

Jen could tell that Grams was trying her best not to show her embarrassment. She had to give her credit—with Jen's training, Grams was growing more and more flappable every day.

"You're going to train to be a lifesaver. You're going to be learning valuable skills like CPR," Grams said. "That class is not a fashion show, and it is certainly not a place to flaunt your anatomy."

Jen stifled a laugh, but before she could respond, a loud knock sounded on the front door downstairs. "Who could that be at this hour?" Grams asked, then charged downstairs in a huff.

Jen walked to her bedroom window and drew aside the curtain. Pacey, clutching a paper bag, was peering into the window next to the front door. After checking herself out in the mirror once more, Jen tugged a pair of shorts and a tank top on over her suit, stepped into her sandals, and ran down the stairs.

"I'll get it," Jen offered. "It's only Pacey. He's taking the class with me." She walked past her grandmother to the front door. "And don't worry," she said over her shoulder as she swung open the front door, "I think he's already aware of my breasts."

Pacey flinched at the last sentence, then laughed. For once, Jen thought, she had caught him off guard and he didn't have a clever comeback. "Morning," Pacey said. "Ready for the big day?"

"Let me just grab my bag," Jen said.

Through the screen door, Jen's grandmother

glared at Pacey disapprovingly. "Good morning to you, too, ma'am," he said.

Grams harrumphed, then scowled and disappeared into the kitchen.

"Have a nice day, Grams," Jen called, then followed Pacey into the yard, laughing.

"What's so funny?" Pacey asked.

"It's nothing," Jen said, pausing to pull her hair back into a ponytail. "It's just that I don't know when she last had a nice day. Or if she ever had a nice day!"

Pacey laughed along with her, then opened the paper bag he was carrying. "She's probably grouchy because she hasn't had her morning coffee." He offered Jen a large white cup with a lid. "Latte?"

Jen drew in a deep breath and eagerly grabbed the cup. "I'm an addict. Thanks! How did you know?"

Pacey smiled mysteriously. "I have my ways."

Jen arched an eyebrow at him.

"Okay," Pacey admitted. "Dawson might have mentioned it once. Or twice. Or three or four times. Along with every other detail about your likes and dislikes, thoughts, feelings, et cetera."

Jen punched Pacey in the arm playfully. "Give Dawson a break, Pace. I know he's kind of obsessive compulsive. But I messed everything up—"

"Hey," Pacey interrupted. "I promise not to talk about that dead horse of a relationship if you don't." He stuck out a hand. "Deal?"

Jen smiled. "Deal," she agreed, pumping Pacey's hand eagerly. She didn't want to rehash Dawson stuff anymore. She wanted to move on. Right now she just wanted to be on her own. No boyfriends. No worries.

She and Pacey didn't talk much more as they walked to the town pool, where they would begin their training. But she felt comfortable, knowing she didn't have to force conversation. Jen just strolled down the street, sipping her coffee and enjoying the warm, gentle morning breeze caressing her face.

At this very moment she finally felt that she belonged to Capeside. She had grown used to the little town, and she liked it. Life was less complicated here than in New York, she thought, though Capeside did have its share of mini-dramas.

Jen had managed to avoid personal catastrophes in Capeside—so far. She wanted to keep it that way. She wanted to live a plain, simple, ordinary life, moving at her own pace.

Now here she was, with a comfortable friend, on her way to her summer job, finally living like a normal kid in Anytown, U.S.A. She took a final gulp of her coffee. She just hoped the peace would last.

Joey sat numbly at the kitchen table, only half absorbing her sister's seemingly endless list of things for her to remember while she watched the baby today.

"And throw in a load of wash, if you can. Okay, Joey?" Bess was saying. "Earth to Joey?"

"I hear you!" Joey snapped impatiently. "It's not like I've never baby-sat before." Then she added under her breath, "It's like *all* I do."

Bess turned sharply on Joey. "What did you say?"

Joey looked her sister right in the eye. "I said, 'I

know what I'm doing.' " She knew Bess didn't have the time to challenge her.

"Look," Bess said. "This would be a lot easier if you lost the attitude. I know it's hard on you, but we have to do our best until we can afford to hire a permanent sitter. If you'll watch him until eleven, Bodie will relieve you so you can make it to the restaurant in time for the lunch shift."

"Happy, happy, joy, joy," Joey muttered. Then to deflect her sister's angry stare she quickly added, "You're going to be late." She took Alexander from her sister's arms. "Bye," she said.

Bess gave her son a kiss on the forehead. "Contrary to popular belief, I do appreciate this," she told Joey before she hurried out the door.

Joey looked down into Alexander's sweet face. He was adorable—red-apple cheeks, wondrous blue eyes, and teeny, tiny nose. When he smiled, he looked just like Joey's mother. God, how Joey missed her. If Mom were around, things would be different, she thought.

Why did she have to go and die on them? If Mom were around, she'd be able to pitch in and watch the baby. If Mom were around, who knows, maybe Bess wouldn't have even gotten pregnant. If Mom were around, Joey wouldn't have to break her back working at the Icehouse, scurrying around to feed the demanding and hungry tourists.

If Mom were around, maybe Joey would have a normal carefree summer. She cradled the baby in her arms and sighed wistfully. What did she have to look forward to this summer besides baby-sitting and working?

Well, she was going to the beach with Dawson tomorrow. That was something.

Sunlight streamed through the kitchen window. It looked like a beautiful day out there, and Joey figured there was no reason for her to stay cooped up in the house. "C'mon, kid, we're going outside," she announced to Alexander.

As Joey sat on the front porch, cradling Alexander, she heard a familiar voice singing jump-rope rhymes. It was her eight-year-old neighbor, Clarissa Cummings. Joey waved at the sweet little girl.

Clarissa dropped her jump rope and ran over to Joey, who smiled at her. Clarissa idolized her.

"Hi, Joey," Clarissa said. "Guess how many times I counted on the jump rope today?"

"Hmm," Joey answered, her face a mask of deep concentration. They played this game all the time. Joey always lowballed her first. "One hundred?"

"More," Clarissa said proudly.

Joey guessed again. "Two hundred?"

"Nope," Clarissa said, shaking her head. "Even more."

"Not five hundred!" Joey said. "That's humanly impossible!"

Clarissa laughed. "Six hundred. But I stopped to say hi and to ask you for a favor."

"Anything," Joey said. And she would do anything for Clarissa. If her nephew turned out to be half as nice, she'd be thrilled. Clarissa was the sweetest kid she knew.

"My family is going on vacation tomorrow for two weeks, and I was wondering if you would watch Howard for me," Clarissa asked.

"Howard?" Joey repeated.

"My pet," Clarissa explained.

Joey didn't recall Clarissa having a pet. That was all she needed—to be stuck with a baby, and a job, and a pet for the summer. "I'm sorry, Clarissa, I can't watch your pet," she said. When she saw the disappointment creep onto Clarissa's face, she thought of an excuse. "I'm allergic."

"Allergic? To plastic?" Clarissa asked.

Joey gave Clarissa a puzzled look. "Your pet is plastic? Is it a toy horse or something? In that case—"

"No, it's Howard, my virtual pet," Clarissa explained. "We're going to Europe, and my parents won't let me bring him. They say I'll pay too much attention to Howard and not enough to the sights, whatever that means."

Joey laughed. A virtual pet! She saw a lot of little kids carrying them around. They were key chain fobs that resembled video games. What a relief! "Sure, then! I'll be happy to watch Howard."

Clarissa gave Joey a jug. Thanks. You're the only person I would trust with Howard, anyway. He's been alive for a record 643 years. If you take care of him, I know he'll still be alive when I come back."

"No problem," Joey said. "If I can take care of my nephew, I'm sure Howard will be fine."

Clarissa excitedly darted off. "I'll go get him—and his manual—for you," she called back.

Manual? Joey thought. How complicated could that little piece of plastic be? Alexander squirmed in her arms and let out a whimper. He was hungry again. Joey stood up and carried him inside so she could give him his bottle.

When Joey had calmed Alexander, she put him in his portable seat on the porch. Clarissa came running over with the pet.

"Hey there, Howard," Joey said when Clarissa ceremoniously handed him over. It was a bright pink egg on a key chain, just as she had expected. But she didn't expect the length of the manual Clarissa gave her next. Joey laughed. "This is a joke, right—this manual?"

"No," Clarissa said seriously. "Joey, it's very important that you read it and follow every rule." Her eyes grew earnest. "If you don't, Howard will die! Please don't kill my pet, Joey! He's my best friend!"

"Okay, okay," Joey said hastily. She didn't want two crying kids on her hands! "I'll read it carefully."

"Thank you, Joey," Clarissa said. She stared at Joey with big liquid eyes. "Howard and you are my best friends."

Alexander started to gurgle and cry again. This time his sounds were more than whimpers. They were earsplitting shrieks.

"Have a great vacation," Joey said to Clarissa, as she carried the infant back into the house. Inside, as the baby screamed, she added, "God knows mine is already shot."

Chapter 5

Pacey scoped the crowd gathered outside at the pool, careful to hide behind his dark sunglasses so he didn't appear to be checking anyone out. Not bad, he thought. Of the ten people who were all together, six were girls. He recognized two kids from school, one girl and one guy, but that was all, and they didn't seem to recognize him. He figured that a good portion of these people just spent their summers in Capeside and this was their parents' way of making sure they had something to do all day. The others probably went to private schools.

There were more than a few cute girls. In fact, all of them were hookup material. The one he recognized from school was a petite redhead named Angela something. Then there were two older-looking girls, probably coeds, he guessed. One was a tall, sophisticated-looking brunette. The other seemed to

24

have been born to be a lifeguard: sandy-haired, athletic, tanned, healthy.

That was when Pacey noticed the crowning glory. Twins. Blond twins. They were the only ones who weren't wearing cover-ups or shirts over their bathing suits. And what a shame it would be, Pacey thought, if they covered up those babacious bods. They looked like movie stars or quintessential California girls, except they were in Massachusetts.

"Dawson, you have no idea what you're missing," Pacey said softly.

He sized up the guys—his competition—quickly. Only three others besides him. He recognized one guy, Todd, from school. He was pasty, frail, and wimpy—definitely not a threat. The other guys looked pretty normal. One was nondescript, nothing special, Pacey thought. The other guy looked cool, but Pacey thought he had girlfriend written all over him. He hoped he was right.

A tall, tanned, muscular older man strolled into the crowd and blew a whistle. Great. Pacey grimaced. He could see the girls swooning already.

"I'm Tim," the man said. "I'll be your lifeguard instructor. I want to welcome you all here." He paused, then took off his sunglasses and regarded the students seriously. "I hope you all will be with me by the end of the course. But unfortunately we lose many students along the way."

Lose them? Pacey wondered what that was supposed to mean. Did people actually drop dead from lifeguard training? This guy Tim was obviously joking. Pacey laughed out loud.

Bad move. The instructor stopped and stared right

at him. Silently he marched over. He stopped right in front of Pacey and assumed a stiff military stance.

"What's your name, young man?" he snapped.

"Pacey,' he answered. "Pacey Witter."

"It's not funny, Witter," Tim said. Little droplets of spittle escaped his mouth and flew right into Pacey's face. "Not everyone graduates. In fact, a third of you will fail this course. Some of you won't even make it past today."

"O-okay," Pacey stammered. "When you said 'lose,' I thought you meant that people died from the intense training or something—that's all."

The class erupted into laughter. Tim, though, remained serious. "Practically," he said. "Some students can't hack it and wish they were dead." He turned away from Pacey and spoke out to the quiet crowd. "Let's get this straight right away. If you're here to get a tan, leave now. If you're here to pick up girls or boys, leave now. If you are here because you enjoy *Baywatch*, leave now."

No one moved. "If you are here for any reason," Tim went on, "other than to protect the safety of the Community of Capeside, leave now." Pacey shrank under Tim's withering stare, but he didn't move a muscle or utter another word.

"Good," Tim said. "Today I will give you a pretest. You must pass this in order to continue with training. Is anyone here under fifteen years of age?" Tim again scanned the crowd. No one raised a hand. "Good. Let's get started. Sink or swim!" he bellowed, then laughed at his own joke.

The rest of the morning was spent mostly waiting and watching. Pacey took the opportunity to break the ice with some of the girls, smiling and helping them out, but many of them were afraid to talk, lest they be reprimanded by Tim.

The pretest consisted of swimming 500 yards, first with a breast stroke, then with a crawl, then with a sidestroke. The trainees also had to tread water with their legs only for at least two minutes, which was harder than Pacey thought it would be. Then they had to dive to the bottom of the deep end of the pool, retrieve a heavy brick, and bring it to the surface.

It was fairly easy stuff. Pacey and Jen passed the test without a problem, but one of the boys—Todd, the guy Pacey recognized from school—failed. He could barely swim, even. Pacey wondered why he was there in the first place.

It was a short day, and they were dismissed before lunch. But Tim made a point of letting everyone know that the days of real training would be longer and much more grueling.

He also passed out manuals and informed the trainees that they would be quizzed the next day on the first chapter.

Pacey took his book, feeling secure. No matter how harsh a picture Tough Tim wanted to paint, lifeguarding was going to be a piece of cake. The harder task would be to bag a babe without getting in trouble.

But Pacey had a feeling he could pass that test with flying colors, too.

Dawson fidgeted behind the counter at Screenplay Video. He had cataloged all the returns, straightened and dusted the shelves, and put out all of the new merchandise. Now he had absolutely nothing to do.

Summer at the store was going to be murder. No one rented movies in the summer, especially during the day. Normal people were outside, enjoying the beach and the nice weather. And here he was, pasty white, wearing a dumb black vest, with three hours to go, and absolutely, positively nothing to do except watch a movie. Suddenly that option seemed unappealing to Dawson.

The bells at the front door rang. Great, he thought. Either this person has the wrong store or it's some vampire wanna-be type, some psycho who holes up all day and watches videos. Dawson glanced toward the door.

It was her! The girl he had spotted last night. And here she was struggling to get a double baby carriage through the door. And here he was, Dawson realized, standing behind the counter like a jerk.

He immediately rushed to the door and held it open. "Wait! Allow me," he said gallantly.

The girl pulled in the carriage and smiled. She wore her shiny sandy-colored hair in a long braid that cascaded down her back. "Thank you. It's hard to get through doors with this thing," she said, laughing. "It's the Cadillac of baby carriages—in size only, of course."

Dawson's heart melted at her smile, but he especially liked her adorable accent. He couldn't quite place it. It sounded almost British but not quite. He was dying to know where she was from.

Dawson cooed over the tiny sleeping babies, who

offered the perfect opening for an introduction. "Are these the Barclay twins?" he asked softly, so not to wake them.

"Yes!" the girl answered cheerfully, tossing her braid over her shoulder. "You know the Barclays, then?"

"They live a few doors down from us," Dawson explained. He stuck out a hand. "Hi, I'm Dawson Leery."

The girl shook Dawson's hand eagerly. "And I'm Sheila Billingsley. I'm the Barclay's nanny."

"Welcome to Capeside," Dawson said. He liked her down-to-earth, friendly manner. And he also liked the comfortable but cool way she dressed: a long, flowing printed skirt, a baggy blue T-shirt, and several unique silver rings and bracelets.

"Where are you from?" Dawson asked.

"A little bit of everywhere, actually," the girl answered. "But mainly from Australia."

Australia. It sounded far away and romantic and fun, and Dawson bet that Sheila Billingsley was, too. "I love Australia," Dawson blurted out.

"Have you been there?" Sheila asked, surprised.

Dawson blushed. "No, actually. What I meant was that I love Australian films, like *Strictly Ballroom* and *Muriel's Wedding*."

"I'm impressed," Sheila said, grinning even wider. "Most Americans' knowledge of Australian films doesn't go beyond '*Crocodile Dundee.*'"

"Well, Dawson admitted. "I'm kind of film-obsessed. I mean, I work here and everything. I make my own films, too."

"That's grand," Sheila said. "Then you would be the perfect person to help me today."

"At your service," Dawson said.

Sheila started to describe the type of movie she was looking for. "Something fun, upbeat, for when I'm sitting tonight. Nothing scary," she warned. "I'll be home alone—except for these two guys, of course." She nodded, indicating the twins.

Dawson noticed her lovely green eyes, which had little flecks of gold in them. She had adorable dimples, too. Definite knockout, but in a wholesome way, Dawson noticed. "I can come up with more than enough suggestions," he assured her, but was drowned out by one baby's wail.

"Oh, dear," Sheila said, picking the baby up. She patted and soothed the infant, but then the other started to shriek, too. "I'm afraid they're getting colicky," she said. Balancing one baby in one arm, she lifted the other. She drew both of them to her breast, then rocked and twirled while singing softly and sweetly.

Dawson watched her calming the infants. She seemed so in control, so self-assured. Not the least bit flustered. Her voice didn't even waver as she sang. "You have a nice voice," he commented.

"I hope you don't mind," she told Dawson. "But this is the only way to quiet them."

"Don't be shy," Dawson said. "It's not like you're going to drive any customers away." After a minute the babies were quiet. He was amazed at how she was able to calm them so quickly and easily. When Joey's nephew started to cry, sometimes half a day seemed to pass before he stopped.

The twins seemed to be under Sheila's spell. They weren't the only ones, Dawson thought.

"I better go," Sheila whispered, when she put the twins back into the carriage. "I can come back for a movie another time. Sorry I have to run, but I should really be getting them home now. It was nice meeting you."

"Wait," Dawson said before she turned to go. "Why don't you let me pick out a tape for you. I can drop it by on my way home from work tonight," he offered hopefully. "It would be no trouble at all."

Sheila beamed. "That would be lovely! Thank you. It would make my life so much easier." She gave Dawson another winning smile. "I'll see you tonight, then, Dawson."

"Bye," Dawson said, then ran over to open the door for her.

When the door closed, Dawson pumped a fist into the air. He usually wasn't so forward with girls, but he had liked Sheila instantly. Now he would spend the next few slow hours picking out the perfect video and dreaming of when he'd see Sheila Billingsley's striking face again.

He could tell right away that Sheila was the answer to his problems. Her name did not start with a *J*. And she was different. She seemed mature and responsible, not cranky like Joey or fickle like Jen.

No doubt about it. Sheila Billingsley was definitely going to be the cure for his summertime blues.

Chapter 6

Pacey sat on the living room couch at home flipping through the lifesaving manual. He chuckled at the cheesy drawings and out-of-date photos as he turned the pages. But the book was thick. It seemed there was a lot to learn.

Crash! The book was suddenly knocked out of his hands by a basketball. His brother, Doug, had thrown it. Now he loomed over Pacey challengingly.

"Shouldn't you be out disco dancing to Abba or something? Or does your date have to spend the night with his wife and kids?" Pacey cracked, never one to miss an opportunity to accuse his older brother of being a closet case.

"Har-de-har," Doug said. "C'mon, I'm bored. Shoot hoops with me. I'm in the mood to whup your butt."

"Look," Pacey said. "I don't care what you're

into. But do me a favor and keep *my* butt out of it." He retrieved the manual, which had flown to the other side of the room. "Besides, I can't. I've got to study for a lifeguarding quiz tomorrow."

Doug let out a peal of laughter. "Lifeguarding? You? Now *that's* a funny joke. I don't know what's worse, drowning or having you, with your rancid breath, perform mouth-to-mouth on me."

Pacey didn't answer him. He cracked open the manual and started reading.

"Come on," Doug prodded. "That stuff is cake anyway, although I know that you're a little, shall we say, slow?"

Pacey closed the book. The only way to get Doug off his back was to shoot a few with him. Anyway, Pacey thought, the first chapter did look like cake—it was all about the history of life-guarding and being professional. Nothing too essential, he figured.

"All right," Pacey said, then followed Doug out to the driveway.

It was the same old story. Doug whooped and yelled and cheered for every basket he made. When he won, which Pacey always let him do, because he was all too familiar with the consequences if Doug lost, he strutted around like he was Muhammad Ali or something.

"What a surprise," Doug said, patting Pacey on the back way too hard. "You're a loser once again." He laughed, then ran inside to shower.

Pacey shook his head. He knew there was no way he was ever going to shed the loser label in his family. But it would be a different story at the pool tomorrow.

Pacey Witter the lifeguard was no loser.

When the clock hit the stroke of six, Dawson ripped off his vest. Nellie, the owner's daughter, had shown up on time to relieve him, thank God. Usually she was late. She had tried to engage Dawson in a boring, gossipy conversation, but he cut her short, telling her he had to go.

"Don't tell me you're finally growing a social life, Dawson," Nellie said bitterly.

"I'm not the one working tonight; you are. Now, that's not very sociable, is it?" Dawson answered as he grabbed the three videos for Sheila. He enjoyed watching Nellie's expression sour. "I guess scheduling you at night is Daddy's way of making sure his little girl isn't *too* social, huh?"

"I guess I'm wrong. You're renting videos again I see," Nellie retorted. "Have a blast. Hope you don't get too wild and crazy."

Dawson didn't even answer her as he raced out the door. He hoped Sheila liked the videos he'd chosen. He'd tell her they were a "welcome to Capeside" gift, courtesy of the store. That was partially true: Dawson had paid for them with the money he earned there.

When he stepped outside into the summer night, he felt magic in the air, as if something special was going to happen tonight. A new girl—just when he needed her. He couldn't believe his luck.

Dawson stopped in his tracks on the sidewalk. Calm down, he told himself. He was just dropping videos off for the most beautiful girl he'd ever seen in his life. There was no call for him to get carried away with delusions of romance. For all he knew, she had a boyfriend. For all he knew, she wasn't the slightest bit interested in him.

But this just had to work out! Dawson thought. She was his only hope of moving on with his life.

As he approached the Barclays' house, his heart pounded with excitement. He couldn't help but get his hopes up about her. She seemed so cool.

When Dawson tapped on the front door, Mr. Barclay answered. He invited Dawson in, giving him a hearty handshake. The hall was full of luggage, and Mr. Barclay explained that he and his wife were going on a week-long trip. "I didn't know that Screenplay Video delivered," he said.

Dawson laughed. "We don't, but Sheila here had her hands full today, so I figured I'd help her out and drop these by on my way home."

Mr. Barclay ushered Dawson into the family room, where he found Sheila feeding one of the twins. "Dawson!" she said cheerfully. "I really appreciate this."

"It was no problem at all," Dawson said. "I hope you like what I've chosen." He laid the three videos on the coffee table.

Sheila immediately pointed out one box. "I've been dying to see that one," she said.

"Me too," Mr. Barclay added, "but every time I try to rent it, it's out!"

"Well, you know," Dawson said with mock pride, "I have pull at the video store."

Mr. Barclay laughed then excused himself. "We

have to get going. But stay as long as you'd like, Dawson. I'm glad Sheila's already made a friend."

"Thanks. Have a great trip." Dawson rose and shook his hand once again. "Cute babies!" he called after him.

Sheila finished feeding the twins and smiled at Dawson. "Hey, if you're not busy, would you like to watch the movie with me?"

Dawson smiled so broadly he thought his face might split in half. Just what he had hoped. "Sure," he said, trying to sound casual.

"I'll make popcorn," Sheila offered.

"I'll help," Dawson countered.

He followed her into the kitchen and they talked as they prepared their snack. Dawson asked her a lot of questions; he wanted to know everything about her. He found out that she was eighteen—not so much older than he was. He learned that she had come to live with the Barclays the week before. He discovered that she liked to sing, play the piano, paint, and read biographies of great women.

"What brought you to Capeside?" Dawson asked her as they walked back to the family room.

"The job," Sheila said. "It sounded too good to pass up."

Dawson nodded. "Capeside may be small and kind of corny, but it has everything you need in a small town—a movie theater, video store, good restaurants."

"I think it's wonderful," Sheila said. "I hope to stay for a while."

Dawson's heart leaped at her last statement. He hoped she stayed, too. "So where were you before

Capeside?" he asked. "Or did you come here straight from the Land of Oz."

"Boston," Sheila answered quickly. "I was there briefly."

"Cool!" Dawson said. "Did you hang out at the Commons a lot? I hear there's this great section for good restaurants, called the North End. Was Boston a fun city?"

"Yes," Sheila said vaguely. Then she picked up a video. "Let's slip this in, shall we?"

They watched the movie, mostly in silence, and they both enjoyed it. By the time the movie ended, Sheila had to put the twins to bed. Dawson helped her, and they chatted a little. Sheila wanted to know all about Dawson's films. He was more than happy to fill her in. She even invited him to bring his own films the next night.

After the twins were asleep, Dawson reluctantly said good-bye. He felt really comfortable with Sheila, and he thought she was an amazing person: smart, talented, beautiful, easy to talk to, and startlingly terrific with newborn twins.

He couldn't wait to get to know her better.

Chapter 7

Joey sat on the beach reading a magazine the next morning. She sighed discontentedly. She wished the hot summer sun would burn Dawson up into a tiny little prune. She didn't know what his problem was, but he was acting like a total stranger today. Almost as if he didn't want to be there. Or maybe as if he didn't want to be there with *her*.

Earlier, when Dawson had come to pick her up, he had walked into the house and immediately fussed over the baby. It seemed as if fifteen minutes had gone by before he even noticed that Joey was there. Then, when the baby started crying and Joey tried to calm him, Dawson had said, "You should sing to him. That's what professional nannies do"— like he was some kind of baby expert or something!

When they finally got going, Joey had asked, "Did you bring the Frisbee?"

"Oh, sorry, I forgot," was Dawson's response.

Joey had specifically asked him to bring it, so what was Dawson's problem? But Dawson was so deep into another galaxy that he claimed she had said no such thing.

To top it all off, on the walk to the beach, Dawson had blathered about this Australian girl he'd met. "Her name is Sheila, and she's from Australia. You should hear her accent—it would sound great on film. She's really photogenic, and she's doing a great job of taking care of the Barclay twins. Maybe she could give you some pointers." And on and on and on.

He had finally stopped talking about Sheila, and now Joey and Dawson sat silently on the beach, Dawson catching some rays, Joey pretending to be engrossed in her magazine, grateful for the silence.

Joey saw Dawson notice the virtual pet hanging from her beach bag. He lifted the little pink egg. "Why do you have one of these things?" he asked.

"That's Howard," Joey responded, looking up from her magazine. "You know Clarissa, my next-door neighbor?"

Dawson nodded.

"She's away in Europe with her family, and she asked me to watch it for her. I said okay, but this thing is kind of a pain. I had no idea until I read the instructions that it had to be constantly monitored. I'm not even sure how to work it."

Dawson laughed again. "Hey, you might learn something from it. It would be good practice for caring for your nephew."

That ticked Joey off. "I get more than enough

'practice,' Dawson, from the real-life baby. It seems like all I do is baby-sit."

"I was just saying—" Dawson began.

Joey threw her magazine down in frustration and cut him off. "You know, it's not my fault that Bess got pregnant. I don't know why I'm the one saddled with all the responsibility."

Dawson held his hands up in defense. "Whoa! I was just making an inane comment. Touchy subject, huh?"

"Like you wouldn't believe," Joey answered. She noticed that a group had started a pick-up volleyball game over at the net. She tried to tune Dawson out by watching the game, but he was being so annoying that it was impossible.

"But it must be hard for Bess," Dawson was saying. "I'm sure it's not easy being a mom and working and looking after her sullen teenage little sister." He lifted his eyebrows.

Joey could tell that Dawson was in lecture mode. "You should cut her a break and help out a little more," he added.

Joey was furious. Dawson was being such a jerk! "When is someone going to cut *me* a break? That's what I want to know!"

But Dawson didn't stop. He went right on with his unsolicited oration. "You know Sheila, the Australian girl I was telling you about?"

How could I not know her? Joey thought. This was the sixth or seventh time he'd brought her up in the past hour.

Dawson went on. "She has to care for newborn twins. *Twins,* Joey. And she makes it seem like it's no sweat. And she's only two years older than we are. It's mind-blowing."

Your mind is blown! Joey thought. She'd had it with Dawson. She didn't feel like listening to him anymore. She didn't even like looking at him. She stood up. "Look, Dr. Spock," she sneered. "I'm going to watch the volleyball game. Keep an eye on Howard, would ya?" She gave him a phony smile and stomped away to the game in progress.

Joey found a grassy spot on a dune to sit and watch the game. She fumed inwardly as she watched the two teams dive, lunge, and scramble for the ball. She tried to follow the game, but she couldn't get Dawson and his stupid lecture out of her mind.

Maybe she *should* help her sister a little more. At the very least, she guessed she could try to "lose the attitude," as Bess had said. But no one seemed to care that Joey was growing up and had no sign of a social life, outside of an occasional video in Dawson's bedroom.

"You want to step in for me?" a panting girl asked Joey.

"Sure," Joey said. Maybe a good hard workout was just what she needed.

In no time it was her turn to whack the volleyball across the net. She slammed it as if it were Dawson Leery's head. Power shot! She looked across the net to see where it was going. Oh, my God! She thought. He's gorgeous! On the other side of the net was a total dream guy—blue eyes, brown hair, and a tanned chest to die for! And he was looking at her. Joey quickly looked away, then back again.

He wore blue bathing trunks with Day-Glo Hawaiian flowers down the sides. They were off-beat for Capeside, but Joey liked that. She especially liked the hair stuck up a little on top. He was gorgeous but a little disheveled, almost like he didn't know how incredibly hot he was. He was smiling at her again. Joey nervously smiled back. What if he was smiling at the girl behind her?

After the game was over, Joey jogged back to her blanket. Her frustrations were at bay after playing volleyball, and she felt a lot better.

Dawson wasn't at the blanket. Joey spied him walking toward the water to take a swim. Hadn't she asked him to watch her stuff? What a space case!

Joey was pretty tired from the game, so she stretched out on the blanket and closed her eyes. The sun felt great, beating down on her. Soon she'd have to leave and get ready for work. What a bummer. She didn't want to move.

She nearly drifted into a nap. The sounds of the waves beating against the beach, the gulls squawking overhead, the . . . beeping? She sat bolt upright. Where was that annoying sound coming from?

Howard. Howard was beeping. She took the egg and peered at the screen. It didn't tell her anything. There was a splotch on one corner of the screen, and in another corner a figure that looked like a duck was flashing.

What in the world did that mean? What kind of genius could decipher these bizarre symbols, anyway? As she dug through her bag for her instruction manual, she noticed that the cute guy from the volleyball game was staring at her.

Joey was ready to die. How was she going to shut this thing up? She wanted to dig a huge hole in the sand and disappear. The guy in the Hawaiian shorts probably thought she was a total dork! Not to mention that everyone else in the immediate area was glaring at her.

She continued to grope for the manual. She knew it was in her bag somewhere, under the extra towel, the water bottle, the sunscreen, and her magazine. Her fingers found the booklet, and she frantically leafed through it as Howard continued to beep.

"It's easier if someone shows you," she heard a voice say. Joey looked up to see Mr. Hawaiian Shorts standing right over her, a pearly white smile on his face.

Before Joey could say anything, he crouched down next to her. "May I?" he asked, gently touching her hand.

"Please," Joey said, maybe a little too eagerly. Up close, Joey noticed what great biceps he had. She handed the virtual pet to him.

"When you see this duck flashing, it means the pet pooped," he said, laughing. "So you have to press this button here to clean it up. Then the flashing stops." The annoying beeping finally ceased, too.

Joey smiled shyly. "Thanks," she said. "I hope it didn't disturb you too much."

"Not at all," he said, handing the pet back to her. "I'm Jeremy, by the way. Jeremy Fields."

"Joey Potter." She laughed. "Why on earth do you know so much about virtual pets, Jeremy Fields?" she asked with another smile.

"I don't get out much," he answered, sitting down in the sand.

Joey laughed again. Looking closely, Joey noticed a dusting of freckles beneath the tan on his smooth, well defined chest. She thought they were adorable.

"The truth is, my younger brother has like five or six of those things," he admitted. "Half the time I get stuck caring for them."

"This belongs to my next-door neighbor," Joey offered. "And it's the first—and last—time I'm going to do this for her. Where are you from?" Joey asked, figuring he was a summer tourist.

"New Hampshire," Jeremy answered. "And you?"

"Capeside—born and bred," Joey said.

Jeremy leaned on an elbow. "I like it here. It's my first time. I'm here on vacation with my parents, my brother, *and* cyberpets of all shapes, sizes, colors, and sounds. I think I could get used to this place." His voice trailed off. "And I guess I'd better take off—looks like your boyfriend is coming back," he said, sitting up.

Joey turned her head to see a dripping wet Dawson approach the blanket. "Him?" she said, laughing. "He's not my boyfriend. I don't have a boyfriend—right now, that is," she added hastily, in case he thought she was a total loser. Oh, God, she was making it worse.

"Well, in that case, are you free for a movie tonight?" Jeremy asked as he stood.

"Sure," Joey said. "I have to work, but I get off at nine, if that's okay," she said as Dawson sat down on the blanket. Jeremy introduced himself to Dawson, but Dawson was ice-cold.

"So," Jeremy said, breaking the tension. "Where should I pick you up?"

Joey gave Jeremy directions to the Icehouse as Dawson sat there glaring.

"See you later, Joey. Nice to meet you Dawson," Jeremy said, before walking back to his blanket.

"Nice shorts," Dawson mumbled. Then he shot Joey a cross look. "Who was that guy?"

Joey, her mood transformed, explained. "He was playing volleyball. Really nice—helped me with this stupid pet."

Dawson stared at Joey in amazement. "You mean you're going to go out with him, just like that?"

"Why not?" Joey challenged. What had gotten into Dawson? First he acted like he'd rather be anywhere in the world but at the beach with her, then he copped an attitude when she made a date with another guy. Could he possibly be jealous? Good! Joey thought with glee.

"I guess you're not coming to movie night, then," Dawson said.

Joey chuckled. Did Dawson actually think she would pass up a date to sit in his bedroom and watch *E.T.* for the five hundredth time? "No. I guess not."

"That's okay, because I had to cancel anyway," Dawson said. "I made plans with Sheila tonight."

"Good," Joey said. "For you."

"Fine," Dawson stated. "Have fun. I just hope this guy isn't some psycho or anything. I mean, he's a perfect stranger."

Joey laughed. " 'Perfect' is right," she quipped. "I hope he won't be a stranger for long."

Chapter 8

Jen sat on the back porch waiting for Pacey. They had decided to walk to class together every day— make it a morning ritual.

It was a beautiful Friday. Once again Pacey brought her a latte. And once again Jen was grateful. "You don't have to do this every day," she said, taking the big white cup. "You'll spoil me."

"You're already rotten," Pacey joked. "I can't do much more harm."

Jen was eager to get to know Pacey better. She'd known him only through Dawson, and she was glad to make her own connection with him.

These days she needed friends. She knew that Dawson was having a hard time trying to be just friends with her. And Joey certainly wasn't making any friendly overtures. So it felt good to be making a bona fide friend.

As they walked to the pool, Pacey made Jen laugh with his "Tough Tim" imitation, complete with spittle. Pacey puffed out his chest. "If anyone here wants to go in the water, leave. If anyone here can't take a little spit in his face, leave. If anyone here is not a bullying macho ignoramus, leave!"

Jen laughed and nearly choked on her coffee. "I think he was probably a lifeguard in Nam or something," she said.

"Or maybe in Alcatraz," Pacey added. "Or maybe he was the Ty-D-Bol man, but he let the promotion go to his head."

They arrived at the pool just in time, luckily. One of the other trainees wasn't so fortunate. He arrived a minute late and was promptly chewed up and spit out by Sergeant Tim.

"I will not tolerate tardiness or absenteeism," Tim bellowed. "During training you are to show up promptly every day. That means Saturday and Sunday too." He ordered them all to sit, accentuating the point by blowing his whistle.

Jen stiffled a giggle. This guy was like something out of a bad television show. But she sat quietly and listened as Tim went through the bylaws of lifeguarding.

"Number one," he said as he marched through the crowd, sizing everyone up, "a lifeguard is humble. He or she does not revel in glory after a rescue."

Pacey and Jen exchanged smirks but grew serious again when Tim neared them. "Number two," Tim went on, twirling his whistle, "a lifeguard will do his best to prevent all dangers and accidents. Number three, a lifeguard is dignified and never abuses his authority."

Jen could hear Pacey choke on those. Tim was the antithesis of all of these statements. "Number four," Tim continued, "a lifeguard acts as a member of a team. He or she does not act for individual gain. He or she follows orders from superiors."

When Tim turned his back, Pacey muttered sarcastically, "Yes, sir," and several people giggled.

Tim whipped around, his steely eyes pinning the group. "Do we have a comedian in our midst?" he said, stomping over to the offending trainees. "If you think you are here to crack jokes, leave now. I will not tolerate humor. Of any kind. At any time. You are training to save *lives*, here. It is no laughing matter. Is that clear?"

The class remained silent. Pacey was grateful that Tim hadn't realized he had cracked that joke.

"I said, is that clear?" Tim repeated.

"Yes," the class chorused.

"Good," Tim said. He went on. "Number five, a lifeguard has a clean and neat appearance. Number six, a lifeguard has a cool head and uses good judgment. Number seven, a lifeguard is prompt and always alert."

Tim stopped pacing and sat down in a plastic chair to finish barking out the bylaws. "Number eight, a lifeguard is always prepared. Number nine, a lifeguard is responsible. And Number ten, a lifeguard is always honing his or her skills."

Tim paused and stared at the uncertain faces before him. "Any questions?"

One of the twins raised her hand. "Yes," Tim said,

picking up a clipboard and looking at a chart. "Mallory or Mindy?"

"I'm Mallory," the girl answered. "Is this going to be on a test?" she asked.

Jen looked at her. What a dumb question. She hated when people were only concerned about learning because of the possibility of tests.

"As a matter of fact," Tim answered, "if you remember, you're going to have a quiz today on chapter one. You will be tested on everything, and I mean everything you learn in this course. You must know all of the information inside out. You will have written tests and performance tests. You will be tested on lifeguarding philosophy and on rescue skills, including artificial respiration." Tim paused dramatically. "I will give you every test imaginable.

"After a few weeks of this class, you will need to take a separate course in CPR," Tim continued. "Then and only then will you get your lifesaving certification. *If* you pass."

"But the summer will be almost over by then!" Pacey protested.

"Right," Tim said. "Then you will assist a lifeguard for the remainder of the season. You will not become a full-fledged lifeguard until next summer."

Pacey felt incredibly let down. Tim had burst his aquatic bubble. His visions of performing mouth-to-mouth on bikini-clad women dissolved. Ideas of heroic acts, such as saving a child or fighting off a man-eating shark, fizzled. Notions of sitting in an elevated chair, being adored and idolized by teenage girls faded away. All images of attaining the perfect savage tan were kaput. If I'd wanted to go to summer school, Pacey thought, I wouldn't have worked so hard for that D in geometry. But his eyes moved from the petite redhead to the twins to the college girls, and he decided that the lifesaving class did have some saving graces after all.

The class spent the rest of the morning listening to Tim's lectures, then taking the quiz. Jen felt fidgety and hot and sweaty, but she had to admit that the information, despite its militaristic presentation, was interesting and valuable. She thought the quiz was a breeze, but she noticed that Pacey didn't seem to be having an easy time with it. She knew he wasn't much of a student, but the chapter had taken a mere twenty minutes to read.

When they were dismissed for lunch, the entire class seemed to breathe a collective sigh of relief.

Jen turned to Pacey, who a minute before had been sitting next to her. But he was gone. She looked around and saw him talking with the twins. Some of the other kids were pairing off and walking to the food stand. She walked toward Pacey and lingered, not wanting to interrupt his conversation.

"Yeah, I would have brought my motorcycle, but it's in the shop. So I guess we're stuck here for lunch. Want to join me?" Pacey was saying.

Motorcycle? What a line, Jen thought. But she noted that the twins seemed more than happy to join him. "Uh, you guys getting something to eat?" Jen asked them timidly. But Pacey and the twins walked off, apparently not having heard her.

Jen couldn't help feeling hurt.

*   *   *

"You certainly have an extra spring in your step today," Bodie teased Joey at the Icehouse later that day.

Joey laughed. "I had a good day at the beach today. I think I'll make a habit of relaxing before I come here."

"Miss!" someone shouted from a nearby table. Joey rolled her eyes and rushed over.

Funny, she thought, as she wiped up a messy spill that a customer had made. Usually, this type of thing would ruin her day. But since she'd met that Jeremy guy, nothing could kill her good mood.

Except maybe Bess. She called Joey over. "Are you going straight home after work tonight?" she asked.

Joey cut her off before Bess could elaborate. "I can't baby-sit tonight. I have a date," she said impatiently.

Bess arched her eyebrows in surprise. "A date? That's terrific. Who's the lucky guy?"

Joey softened when she saw that her sister was truly interested and happy. "Someone I met at the beach today. A total hunk."

"Great," Bess said, patting her little sister on the back. "Have a terrific time."

"I'm sorry I can't help out tonight," Joey added apologetically.

Bess waved the worry away. "I don't need you to baby-sit. I was just going to give you money to give to the sitter before I got home. She can wait."

"Oh," Joey said. She felt bad for snapping the minute her sister asked her a question. "Well, you'll probably meet Jeremy, then. He's going to pick me up here tonight."

"Good, then I can warn him before he gets in too deep," Bodie cracked as he passed by. Joey flicked a wet towel at him and laughed.

Sometimes, she thought, this poor excuse for a family was okay.

Jen munched on her burger. Alone. Two tables away from Pacey. She thought about getting up and moving to another table because she didn't know how much longer she could listen to him and his harem of fans. Even though she wasn't right next to him, she could hear every last detail of his conversation—actually, monologue was more like it.

She felt as if she'd been dumped. Jen knew that was ridiculous, but she couldn't help it. Dumped by Pacey, just when she thought they might be good friends. She understood that he wanted to meet new girls, and she didn't want to ruin his rap. But did he have to totally ignore her? And did he have to act like such a jerk?

"Well, after the shark attack, that's when I decided I wanted to train to be a lifeguard," he was saying.

Jen shook her head. He was making up all these preposterous stories to impress the girls. And they were falling for it, egging him on with oohs and aahs and questions. Even the guys at that table were looking at him and nodding with respect. What was with Pacey's Jekyll and Hyde act? Jen wondered. How could someone so sweet turn into such an imbecile in just one day?

She finished her burger and carried her tray over to the trash bin. When she walked past Pacey's table, his audience was roaring with laughter. Jen couldn't resist. She had to go over.

"Hey," she said, pleasantly enough. "What's so funny?"

Pacey looked like a deer caught in headlights. Mallory—or was it Mindy?—said, "Pacey was just telling us about the time that he met that famous DJ and told him off." She giggled.

Pacey's look acknowledged that Jen was the only person who could bust him. But she didn't want to do that. She just wanted to see him squirm a little.

Jen gave Pacey a meaningful glance and then laughed. "Oh, yeah," she said. "That was a good one. I should know—I was there," she lied. Instantly she saw the relief and gratitude in Pacey's eyes.

Jen grabbed a seat at the table and looked at her watch. They still had ten minutes to kill before they had to report back to class. "So tell me, when is that motorcycle of yours getting out of the shop?"

Pacey shrugged and mumbled something about the difficulty of finding a good mechanic these days.

Jen didn't challenge him. She'd saved him this time, she thought. But she wouldn't be so gallant in the future. No way.

Chapter 9

*D*awson checked himself out in the mirror. He looked okay—no zits, at least. He slapped on a dab of cologne, afraid to put on too much like his dad's friend Ed. His family liked to joke that they could always smell Ed coming.

Then Dawson gathered his tapes and his camera and ran down the stairs, in a hurry to get to Sheila's house. He nearly bowled his father over on his way out the door.

"Whoa!" Mr. Leery said, putting his hands out before him. "Where's the fire, kiddo?"

"Only in my heart, Dad," Dawson answered poetically. "I'm going over to the Barclays'."

Mr. Leery threw Dawson a funny look. "What's at the Barclays'?"

"Only the most beautiful, amazing, stupendous, incredible woman I've ever met," he said.

Mr. Leery shifted uncomfortably. He looked around awkwardly, his face growing serious. "Isn't she a little old for you, son?" he asked quietly.

Dawson stared at his dad, surprised. Usually he was so supportive. Sheila was only a little older, for God's sake. "She's not that much older, Dad," he said defensively, then added, "What difference does age make, anyway, in a great romance?"

Dawson wanted to bolt, but his father put a hand on his shoulder, then cleared his throat and scratched his chin. "Well, let me put it this way, then." He hesitated. "Isn't she a little *married* for you, son?"

Dawson stared at his father, stunned for a second. Then he broke into laughter. His dad obviously thought he meant Mrs. Barclay. As Mr. Leery watched Dawson, perplexed, Dawson tried to catch his breath. "Dad, you've got it wrong," he was able to get out, finally. "I'm not going to see Mrs. Barclay. I'm going to see Sheila, their new nanny."

"Oh, huh, huh," Mr. Leery said, half laughing, half embarrassed. "I wasn't aware of the new boarder in the Barclay household. Give me the details!"

Dawson usually loved to sit and chat with his dad, but right now he just wanted to get to Sheila's. Tonight he was going to show her his movies. He didn't want to be a minute later than he had to. "Listen, Dad," he said politely, "I'll give you details another time, okay?"

Mr. Leery good-naturedly punched his son in the arm. " 'Kay. Have a good time."

When Dawson stepped outside, he noticed that

the moon was full. Its brightness was startling, throwing a magical glow upon the creek. It reminded him of that romantic movie, *Moonstruck*. Coincidence? Dawson thought. Not likely. But hopefully Sheila would be the Cher to his Nicholas Cage before long.

Dawson quickened his pace. He couldn't get to Sheila's fast enough. It had been a long day, and he needed to get his mind off things. Things like Joey.

What was with her today? With that guy at the beach, a total stranger, she had acted all goofy and giddy and flirty, whereas she had chastised Dawson for forgetting the Frisbee, and she'd thrown a tantrum when he mentioned Bess and the baby.

Which reminded him—she was going out with that guy tonight. A knot twisted in his stomach at the thought. He hoped the guy wasn't some kind of psycho. Though he did seem all right at the beach—despite his shorts, Dawson mused.

But still, something didn't feel right about it. Something didn't feel right about Joey *dating*.

When he arrived at the Barclays', Dawson decided to leave all thoughts of Joey and her date at the door. Thanks to Sheila, however, that was nearly impossible.

"Hello, Dawson," Sheila said.

At the first sight of Sheila's smiling face, Dawson felt better about everything. She seemed so genuinely pleased to see him—unlike Joey today at the beach.

And Sheila showed a genuine interest in Dawson's films. It felt nice to have a new and interested audience. All of Dawson's friends seemed indifferent to his projects and efforts. When he tried to talk to them about new ideas or techniques, they all seemed to be stifling mammoth yawns. Sheila, on the other hand, was attentive and inquisitive and, best of all, impressed.

Dawson felt comfortable and relaxed for the first time in days, was he popped a tape into the VCR and sat on the couch. He was fine—until Sheila asked a disturbing question. In the middle of the monster film she pointed to Joey and asked, "Is she your girlfriend?"

Dawson laughed uncomfortably. "No! That's Joey. She's just a friend. We've known each other since we were little," he explained.

"She's pretty," Sheila added.

"I guess," Dawson hedged. "I mean, if that's your type. There's a really good scene coming up," he added, trying to change the subject.

But Sheila wouldn't let it go. "Is Joey *your* type? Do you like her?"

Dawson didn't understand why she was prodding. He didn't want to talk about Joey, of all people, when he was trying to get to know someone new. Was Sheila feeling out his romantic status? If so, he was going to make it perfectly clear that he was unattached and looking.

Sheila watched Dawson expectantly. He realized he hadn't answered her question. "My type? We're just friends. I've never thought about it," he lied.

"It's just that I thought I saw something there," Sheila went on.

Though Dawson desperately wanted to change

the subject, he couldn't resist asking, "What do you mean?"

"The way you project her—the roles you write for her. She's always a smart and capable heroine, at least in the movies you've shown me. It's like you respect her—put her on a pedestal, almost. And the way she looks at the camera, at you . . ." Her voice trailed off. "I guess I'm just being silly," she conceded.

"Yeah, I guess," Dawson answered, embarrassed.

There was an awkward pause, but they both re-laxed as they continued watching the film.

Sheila spoke when the film was over. "Does Joey star in all of your films?" she asked playfully. "Many directors fall in love with their lead actresses, you know."

"Yeah, yeah," Dawson said. "Woody and Mia. Cassavetes and Rowlands. The list goes on." He waved an impatient hand at her. "But that's not the case here at all. Joey and I are just friends."

"Okay," Sheila said, then added teasingly, "If you say so."

Dawson popped in another tape. He wondered as they sat on the couch, nearly touching, if he should lean over and kiss Sheila—show her that his mind wasn't on his leading lady after all.

He turned and admired her pretty profile, her smooth, healthy complexion. But oddly, something held him back: he didn't *want* to kiss her.

Dawson couldn't believe it. Something felt weird. Something was missing.

Why? he wondered desperately. Why was this happening to him now?

"How do you keep the camera steady during those action scenes?" Sheila asked, breaking through Dawson's thoughts. "How do you zoom so fast?"

Dawson picked up his camera, happy that she was talking about something else. "Here," he offered. "I'll show you how."

Dawson's mood lightened when he demonstrated some of his favorite camera techniques. They took turns filming each other.

Sheila filmed Dawson from different angles. She giggled when Dawson made funny faces to the camera. He enjoyed filming Sheila just as much: Sheila holding the babies. Sheila singing. Sheila doing a cartwheel outside in the moonlight. Sheila playing the piano.

Fooling around with the camera on Sheila gave Dawson an idea: the documentary—he could practice documentary technique on Sheila. Why not? He thought. He could shadow her, filming her with the babies, adding a few snippets about an Australian living abroad. The story angle would be great practice.

It would also give him an opportunity to get to know her better. If he spent more time with her, he was bound to feel a spark. Once he felt more comfortable around her, he wouldn't feel so awkward if he wanted to steal a kiss.

"How about if I shadow you for a day?" Dawson asked, excited about the idea.

"Shadow me?" Sheila repeated. "I don't know what you mean."

"Don't worry, it doesn't mean 'stalk,' " Dawson

explained. "I would just film you as you work. It would be great practice for my next project—a documentary. I could practice with *A Day in the Life of a Young Australian Nanny.*"

Sheila hesitated a bit. "I'm pretty camera shy, but if it would help you . . . It's just for practice, right?" she confirmed.

"Yes," Dawson said. "Practice."

"Okay, then," Sheila agreed. "Why don't you come on Sunday? Early. These two get up at the crack of dawn."

"Great!" Dawson said. "Maybe we can take them to the beach or something, get a few scenery changes."

"Sounds marvelous," Sheila said in her Australian lilt. She looked at her watch. "Right now I'm afraid I have to get these two peanuts to bed."

Dawson took the cue and gathered up his tapes and camera. "Okay, then. Sunday." He paused at the front door. "Thanks for inviting me over. I had a great time tonight," he told her.

Sheila grinned. "Ditto. You feel like an old friend, Dawson Leery."

An old friend. More like a comfortable old shoe. That was exactly what Dawson had been afraid she would think.

Chapter 10

The last few customers lingered in the Icehouse on the warm, breezy Capeside night. As Joey bussed a table, she thought her stomach would burst with excitement by the time nine o'clock rolled around.

Bess walked over and helped Joey clear the table. "Why don't you knock off a little early?" she said. "Get pretty for your hot date."

Joey happily untied the strings of her apron. "Thanks, Bess," she said. "I'll put in some extra time tomorrow."

She walked to the back room and unzipped a duffel bag. She pulled out a change of clothes and a small makeup case. Joey didn't usually wear a lot of makeup. In fact, she had nice coloring from her time at the beach that day. But she did want to brush her hair, put on a bit of lipstick, and maybe borrow a dab of perfume from her sister.

She pulled off her food-stained jeans and changed into her outfit for the night: black pants and a silvery halter top. She dressed the ensemble up with a silver chain, then regarded herself in the mirror, pleased at what she saw. She hoped Jeremy would like her style.

Precisely at nine, Joey perched on a stool at the bar. She grabbed some menus to stuff with flyers announcing house specialties for the next day so she wouldn't seem to be waiting with bated breath, which she was.

After a minute, Bodie approached her and whistled. "Hello, foxy lady. Have you seen Josephine?" he asked. "There's someone here to see her," he said.

Joey whirled around and saw Jeremy, clutching a dozen roses, scanning the Icehouse. Joey smiled and waved him over.

As he walked toward her, Bess stopped him and introduced herself. They chatted for a minute, and Joey was pleased to see her sister's approving smile.

Jeremy looked neater than he had at the beach. His hair was combed, and his clothes were neatly pressed. He wore a casual, colorful bright blue shirt with comfortable light tan pants.

Jeremy smiled as he strolled over. He stopped before Joey and thrust out the roses. "Hi," he said. "Uh, these are for you."

Was that a hint of nervousness she heard in his voice? She liked that, too. She was starting to think she liked everything about Jeremy Fields.

"Thanks," Joey said shyly as she took the bouquet

from him. No boy had ever given her roses before. "They're pretty," she said.

"Like you," Jeremy said. "You look really pretty tonight."

Joey blushed. She wasn't used to being complimented in that way. But she didn't want to seem like a flattery-flustered airhead. "Plastic surgery pays off," she said. "Everyone says it's a major improvement from before the kitchen fire."

Jeremy laughed. "Well, then, I feel more comfortable telling you about my artificial baboon heart, then," he said.

Quick comeback, Joey thought. He thinks on his feet. Another great quality. "We should get going," she told him, "if we want to make the movie on time. Just let me put these in water—"

"Taken care of," Bess said, popping up behind Joey and grabbing the roses from her hand.

Joey felt a twinge of guilt. Bess always seemed to be there when she needed her. Was Joey there for Bess as much? Yes, Joey thought. She did more than her share to help Bess—at home and at the restaurant. It was nice to know, though, that Bess returned the favors.

They walked to the theater, which was just down the road from the Icehouse. "So do your parents own the restaurant?" Jeremy asked to make conversation.

Joey froze up inside. She knew it was an innocent question, but he had no idea what a can of worms he was opening up when he mentioned her parents.

"Um, well, my Mom died, and my Dad left," Joey

said, fibbing slightly. She figured that Jeremy didn't have to know that her dad was in jail.

Jeremy looked concerned. "I'm sorry," he said.

Joey shrugged. "So Bess and I own the restaurant, I guess," she said. "We're the sad excuse for the Potter family: me, my sister, her live-in boyfriend, and their child." Joey watched Jeremy's face carefully for a reaction.

He didn't seem the least bit fazed. "So you're not the Brady Bunch," Jeremy said. "Your sister and her boyfriend seem pretty cool. They've got to be more tolerable than my mom and dad."

"Which rerun TV family did you always wish was yours?" Joey asked. "I always wanted to be one of the Keatons on *Family Ties*."

Jeremy laughed. "Why? They were so corny!"

"But they seemed so happy," Joey countered. "The Keatons seemed so normal." She felt comfortable with Jeremy, making easy conversation. But at the same time, being near him sent tiny shivers up and down her arms.

Jeremy thought about Joey's question. "I always wanted to be one of the Munsters," he said.

Joey laughed. "You're not serious," she said.

"I am," Jeremy insisted. "I always wanted to be in *The Munsters* because I had a crush on Marilyn, the normal cousin."

That put Joey in stitches. She liked his sense of humor.

"I've been looking forward to seeing this movie," Joey said as they approached the ticket window. "I hope you're into it. Dinky little Capeside only has one theater, so we don't have much choice."

"Sounds like my town in New Hampshire," Jeremy said. "One movie theater. One grocery store. One school. Hundreds of people dying to get out."

They hurried into the theater when Joey noticed the time.

"I know you'll think this is weird," Jeremy said. "But I like to sit in the front row. No one ever sits there and it has the most leg room."

Joey giggled. She'd never thought of it that way. She was game for the front row. They walked toward the screen just as the previews started to roll.

But as soon as they sat down, Jeremy raced out to get some snacks. "I'll be back," he told her, doing his best Terminator impression.

After a couple of minutes, Jeremy returned with a big bucket of popcorn. When he offered her some, Joey declined. She was a little hungry, but movie-theater popcorn always gave her a stomachache. But Jeremy had no way of knowing that. It was the thought that counted, she told herself.

Jeremy cocked an eyebrow when Joey passed up the popcorn. "I suppose you'd be interested in some of these, then," he said, slowly sliding a box of Sno-Caps out of his shirt pocket. He gave her a knowing smile and chuckled.

Sno-Caps were Joey's favorite. "How did you know?" she asked, making a grab for them.

"Your sister tipped me off," Jeremy confessed.

Sno-Caps, a good movie, and a cute guy, Joey thought. What more could a girl ask?

*　　*　　*

Dawson quietly opened the door and walked into the living room. His parents were snuggled up on the couch, watching a movie. "What are you watching?" Dawson asked.

Dawson's mother hit the pause button. *"When Harry Met Sally,"* she answered. "Do you want to watch it with us?"

"No," Dawson answered abruptly. "I've seen it." I *live* it, he thought.

He abruptly wished his parents good night and climbed the stairs to his bedroom. What a night, he thought as he plopped onto his bed. He'd had a great time with Sheila, but why had they spent so much time talking about Joey? And why had he spent most of the night thinking about Joey? He turned his TV on, not ready to go to sleep. He thought he might dream about Joey if he did.

Dawson took the tape he'd made tonight and popped it in the VCR. Sheila's smiling face came up on the screen. Now *that's* who you should be dreaming about, he told himself.

He stopped the tape when there was a tap at his door. "Come in," Dawson called.

His mother opened the door a crack. "We're done watching the movie," she said. "Are you okay?" she asked tenderly.

"Yeah," Dawson answered.

"You seemed to run up here so quickly," his mother explained. "That's not like you."

Leave it to his parents to notice every emotion he had. Sometimes he thought they had X-ray vision that pierced right into his psyche. "I just made this tape, and I was anxious to watch it," Dawson said. "That's all."

"Oh." His mom sat on the corner of his bed. "Not soft porn, I hope," she joked.

Dawson laughed. "Just hard-core goofing around with the Barclays' new nanny." He played part of the tape for her.

"She's pretty—and charming," Mrs. Leery noted. "And look how good she is with those twins." She cocked her head, as if she were struck by an idea. "How old is she, Dawson?"

"Eighteen," he answered.

"Is this her summer job?" she asked.

"I suppose," Dawson said. "She just started." He didn't understand her sudden interest.

"Perfect!" Mrs. Leery said happily. "I'm doing a TV series on teens and their summer jobs for the station. Do you think Sheila would be interested in being one of my subjects? Her story would give my series the international flair it needs."

Dawson quickly thought it over. Sheila would be perfect. She was beautiful, photogenic, and an all-around amazing person. "I don't see why not," he said. "She would be perfect." In fact, Dawson saw a perfect opportunity. Maybe he could do the piece for his mother. He told her how he planned to shadow Sheila on Sunday.

Dawson's mother balked a bit. "I don't know. Isn't that nepotism?"

"I've got great equipment, and I need the experience," he pleaded. "Plus I am extremely cheap," he added for effect.

Dawson's mother laughed. "You have a great

point there." She considered the idea for another moment. "If my producers approve, you're in," she conceded.

"All right!" Dawson cheered.

Mrs. Leery rose to leave. "But first I need Sheila's written permission to use her as a subject."

"No problem, Mom," Dawson said confidently. "I'll take care of it Sunday."

Dawson's mother kissed him on the forehead and wished him good night. When she closed the door behind her, Dawson turned off the VCR, undressed, and crawled under the covers.

He couldn't wait to tell Sheila about the project. He was sure she would flip. This could be the perfect thing to bring them together.

Dawson shut his eyes, eager to get to sleep. Tonight Dawson was sure to have sweet dreams—very sweet dreams about *The Life and Times of Sheila Billingsley*.

Chapter 11

On the screen a policeman ran down a dank, dark alley. He could barely see. He held his gun out in front of him, ready for anything.

The alley came to a dead end. The criminal had to be in there somewhere. At any minute he could jump, shoot, or—

Beep. The familiar high-pitched sound sent Joey scrambling in her purse.

Howard. He was back.

Beep.

"Hey! Shut that thing off!" someone shouted at her.

Joey retrieved the pink egg and swiftly silenced it.

She breathed a sigh of relief. But then she heard a stifled snort of laughter from Jeremy.

Joey could tell that Jeremy was trying his best to hold it in. But he was sputtering through a mouthful of popcorn. Before she could control it, she was laughing, too.

"Shh!" came from all over the theater. But the harder Joey tried not to laugh, the more she wanted to. She couldn't help it.

She and Jeremy were in the midst of an all-out laughing fit.

Jeremy took Joey's hand and, clasping a hand over his mouth, stood up and raced for the exit.

He pushed open the door, and when they emerged outside, they both let loose.

"What timing!" Jeremy said between guffaws. "That thing needs discipline! I think that little girl spoils it."

Joey wiped tears from her eyes. "Shh! Turn that thing off!" she said in imitation of the annoyed people behind her.

Jeremy took a deep breath and sighed. "I didn't mean to make you miss the movie," he said. "We can go back in."

"No," Joey said. "I wasn't into it anyway. The acting wasn't very good." Even though she hadn't enjoyed the movie, she was having a great time. "I—I haven't laughed like that in a long time," she confessed. And it was true. With Mom gone, and Dad in jail, and with her and Bess and Bodie trying to make ends meet, there wasn't a lot for Joey to laugh about these days. But for a few beautiful moments Jeremy had made her forget.

"If *you* want to go back, though . . ." she said, thinking that Jeremy might want to catch the ending.

Jeremy's expression grew sheepish. "Don't worry

about it," he said casually, then let out a rueful laugh. "I am such a dork," he muttered.

"What?" Joey pressed.

"I've seen the movie already," he blurted. "And I can tell you that it doesn't get any better. I know you're going to think I'm a big loser, but you seemed to really want to see it, so . . ."

Joey grinned delightedly. She thought that was the sweetest thing she'd ever heard. No one ever wanted to see the movies she wanted to see. Dawson—Mr. Film—always seemed to dictate what they would see and when. It was so nice of Jeremy to sit through it a second time for her. "Thanks," she said tenderly.

"What for?" Jeremy asked.

"For sitting through a bad movie again. And especially for making me laugh," Joey told him. She wanted him to know what his kindness had meant to her. "I needed it. Too much."

Before she could say anything more, Jeremy took her hand.

Joey could feel his strength. His sleeve brushed against her bare arm, and her skin tingled. There, right in the middle of the parking lot, his lips brushed hers.

"C'mon. I'll walk you home," he said after a trancelike moment. "Then I'll give you a real goodnight kiss."

And he did.

When they approached her house, Jeremy pulled Joey close and gave her an incredibly sweet, soft, and tender kiss.

Chapter 12

"Morning," Pacey greeted Jen. He strolled up to the back porch, coffee in hand as usual.

"Morning," Jen answered. She accepted her latte and took a sip. She needed to wake up this morning—she felt a little slow and sleepy. But the coffee, along with the chilly New England air, perked her up instantly.

As they walked slowly and silently toward the pool, Jen noticed that Pacey seemed preoccupied. He looked as if he had something important to say, something that might escape his lips at any moment, but he was searching for the right words.

Jen was right. Suddenly Pacey blurted, "Thanks for yesterday." He gave her an uncomfortable nod and shrug.

Jen knew what he was talking about, but she wasn't going to let him off the hook so easily.

"Thanks for what?" she asked, a little too nonchalantly.

Pacey sighed. "You know, at lunch. Helping with my story."

Jen feigned enlightenment. "Oh, you mean thanks for helping you with your big *lies* yesterday."

Pacey grew irritable. He stopped walking. "I knew you'd cop an attitude about this."

Jen opened her mouth, outraged. He should be grateful to her! She could have made him look like a fool in front of the whole class. But she didn't.

She wanted to shake Pacey. Instead she said quietly, "You know, Pacey, you could meet girls by being yourself, too. It's easier. It's hard to keep up a false image. And it will be hell when the lies are peeled away."

Pacey scoffed. "Obviously you're not familiar with my track record as Pacey Witter, major-league mess-up."

"If you don't have faith in who you are, no one else will," Jen insisted. She knew Pacey was insecure. But he was fooling himself. He was a likable guy. Why wouldn't anyone like that?"

Jen could see color rising in Pacey's face. "It's easy for you to say, Miss I'm-So-Self-Assured-and-Beautiful-That-Men-Fight-Over-Me-and-Sulk-About-Me-All-Day," he said quietly. "You have no idea what it's like to be rejected."

Now Jen was getting mad. "You're *wrong*, Pacey," she answered, her voice angry. "I do know. You don't know about my past."

"Right! Exactly!" Pacey said heatedly. "Because you ran away from New York and reinvented yourself here in Capeside. Not everyone gets a second chance. Not everyone gets to move away." He paused, his eyes entreating. "I have a label everywhere I go. At home I'm a disappointment, a failure. At school I'm a joke. Let me have my clean slate. Let me be who I want to be."

"Who do you want to be, Pacey?" Jen asked. She felt a little sorry for Pacey, but she still didn't agree with him.

"Anyone but me," he told her. "Anyone but me."

Pacey looked at the corrected quiz that Tim shoved into his hand. He'd gotten an F. Pacey figured that he shouldn't be surprised. He hadn't read that first chapter the other night. But it was only a quiz, after all. It didn't mean anything in the grand scheme of things, he reasoned.

Pacey saw Jen notice his grade and shoot him a look.

He just didn't get her. Did she think that he wanted to have to lie about who he was? Didn't she get it? No girl who really knew him would like him.

After Tim handed out the quizzes, he turned and faced the class. "Everyone into the pool," he ordered. "Let's see twenty laps—pronto." The class jumped into the water. Then Tim strode out of the area. "I'll be back," he said over his shoulder.

"Probably has to use the john," Pacey muttered.

The minute Tim left, Pacey pulled himself out of the pool. While everyone else was swimming, he decided to entertain the class.

He strutted around the edge of the pool, puffing out his chest in his best Tim imitation. "I am living proof," he shouted, "that size *does* matter. If I didn't have my—shall we say, *shortcomings?*—I wouldn't be the beefed-up bully I am now!"

The students in the pool slowed their laps and laughed, except for Jen. "You should get in the pool, Pace, before he comes back," she warned.

"Why don't you dislodge the life preserver from your butt, young lady?" he barked, again in Tim mode. The crowd lost it, and Pacey basked in the laughter and approval of the class.

He smirked at Jen. She shot him a wounded look.

He had to admit. He felt bad.

He stood at the edge of the pool, frozen, wondering what he should do. Suddenly he felt a hand push him from behind.

A big strong hand.

Tim's hand.

Pacey splashed into the water. When he emerged, coughing, he was staring into Tim's icy eyes.

"I thought I told you to swim twenty laps."

"Yes, sir." Pacey didn't see any way out of this. He treaded water, silently praying that Tim hadn't overheard the mimic show he had put on.

"Then what are you waiting for?" Tim growled.

"Nothing, sir," Pacey answered.

Tim blew his whistle. "Everybody out!" he ordered.

When Pacey started to climb out of the pool, Tim pushed him back in. "Except for you. You swim one hundred laps. Starting now."

Joey felt as if she were floating when she woke that morning. Had the evening before been a dream? It sure seemed like one. But it had been real.

She stretched and yawned, a little tired. It had taken her a long time to fall asleep last night. Between replaying the evening in her mind and being disturbed by her nephew's bawling, Joey was surprised she slept at all.

She had to work today. But tomorrow she would be off, and she was going to spend the day with Jeremy at the beach. Today he was going on a boating trip with his family. She couldn't believe she had to wait a whole day until she saw him again.

It would be torture.

Joey got out of bed and slowly made her way to the kitchen. She found Bess sitting at the table with some orange juice. Joey flinched when she saw the dark circles under her sister's eyes. Bess looked like she hadn't slept in days.

"Little one keep you up?" Joey asked.

Bess nodded. "I'm exhausted."

No kidding, Joey thought. But Bess looked worse than tired. She looked pale. In the summertime, she used to be glued to the beach. Now she looked as if she'd never seen the sun. And her hair, once long and shiny, was dull and frazzled.

"Did you have a good time last night?" she asked wearily.

"Yeah," Joey answered, distracted by how worn-out Bess looked. Was this her sister? Suddenly she seemed twenty years older. And Bess was young, Joey realized. She and Bodie should be going out at night and having fun, like other people their age.

They should be going to the beach, eating at chic restaurants, and checking out local bands.

"I'm going to shower," Joey said abruptly. The sight of Bess had freaked her out. She felt bad that Bess was saddled with this kind of responsibility so young. But then she got mad. It was one thing for Bess to have to take care of Joey—that wasn't her fault. But why did she have to go and get pregnant? She didn't even have time for Joey anymore. Everything revolved around Alexander.

Joey hurried to the bathroom and closed the door behind her. In the shower she closed her eyes and pretended she was somewhere else.

Someplace where there were no worn-out older sisters, no babies who cried in the night, no feelings of guilt bombarding her.

A faraway place where she could hide away with Jeremy Fields.

Chapter 13

Pacey missed lunch. He was busy swimming laps. By the time class ended, in the late afternoon, he was starving. He told Jen to go ahead without him, and he stopped at a pay phone to call Dawson.

He hadn't seen Dawson since he started this dumb class. Maybe Dawson would grab a bite with him.

He put a quarter in the pay phone and dialed. Dawson answered, and Pacey asked him to meet him at the Icehouse. Dawson was more than happy to agree.

By the time Pacey arrived at the Icehouse, Dawson was already there. They grabbed a table, and Joey gave them menus.

"What's up?" Joey asked happily when she saw them.

"*Nada*," Pacey answered.

Joey rushed off to pick up a food order.

"How's lifesaving class going?" Dawson asked as he scanned the menu.

Pacey sighed. "Not what I expected," he admitted. "Screenplay Video is looking better and better."

Dawson laughed. "At least you're outside all day. It stinks being cooped up in that tiny store."

"Yes," Pacey agreed, "but you don't have some neo-Nazi spitting in your face and barking orders at you. And you're not subjected to boring lectures or Jen glowering at you the whole time just because you want to meet some girls."

Dawson put down his menu and gave Pacey his full attention. "Glowering? Jen? Why would she care?"

"Good question," Pacey said. He'd never thought about that. Why *would* Jen care? He paused thoughtfully. "I don't know, man. Maybe she's jealous."

Dawson's face tightened. "Why would she be jealous of *you?*"

Pacey shrugged. "Maybe she has the hots for me?" He laughed, but still, he thought about it. Maybe that was her problem. That would make sense of all those touchy-feely conversations she was having with him about being himself.

"Yeah, right," Dawson said, giving Pacey a dirty look.

"No," Pacey said. "It makes sense. She digs my scene. That's why she doesn't want me to meet other girls!" Pacey shook his head in bewilderment. Why had it taken him so long to notice that Jen Lindley had the hots for him?

Just then he saw Jen walk into the Icehouse. "Whoa, here's my woman now," he said. He waved her over as Dawson shot him a dirty look.

"Hey, guys. Okay if I join you while I wait for my take-out?" Jen asked. She was wearing a short fluttery skirt that showed off her tanned legs.

Pacey gave her a wide smile. "Sure," he said, and gallantly stood and pulled out a chair for her. She did look good. Very good.

"Hi, Jen," Dawson said.

"Hey, Dawson," she answered pleasantly.

Joey came by with some water. She greeted Jen cheerily. "Long time no see!"

Jen appeared surprised at Joey's friendliness. She grabbed a glass and took a sip of water. "Hi Joey," she said. "Yeah, long time no see."

Pacey thought about what he should do. He liked Jen, but he wanted to meet someone new. He figured he ought to let Jen down easy and cut things short before they got started.

"I'm sorry about the life-preserver comment today in class," Pacey said.

"Don't worry about it," Jen said. "I've kinda been acting like a stick-in-the-mud."

Pacey gently patted her hand. "I didn't understand why before, but I get it now."

"I'm glad," Jen answered, taking another sip of water. "I mean, I had no idea what had gotten in to you."

Pacey smiled and nodded. "I didn't mean to—" He stopped. How was he going to put this? "I know you're used to guys making a big fuss over you and stuff. But . . . can we just be friends?"

Jen swallowed another sip of water and gave Pacey a curious look. "What are you talking about?" she asked. "Of course we're friends."

Pacey noticed Dawson's face just then. His expression was a combination of dismay and disgust. Right then it occurred to him that Dawson might not be comfortable with this conversation. Pacey knew he had not completely recovered from his breakup with Jen.

Trying to be tactful, Pacey leaned over confidentially, tipping his head toward Dawson. "Maybe we should have this conversation another time," he said.

"Don't stop on account of me," Dawson said bitterly.

Jen glanced from Dawson back to Pacey. She looked as if she had no idea what was going on. "Here and now is as good a place as any. What's up with you guys, anyway? Am I in the dark about something?"

Pacey went on, "I didn't realize you were jealous, that's all. Forgive me for being so clueless," he said warmly, looking Jen in the eye, "but I'm afraid I think of you only as a friend."

"Jealous?" Jen's eyes widened. "Jealous!" Then she started to laugh hysterically. "That's the stupidest thing I've ever heard! Why would I be jealous?"

"Don't be embarrassed," said Pacey. "I know you're jealous because you have the hots for me. It's okay. But I'm a healthy, young guy. I can't commit myself to one girl right now."

Jen stopped laughing. Her mouth dropped open.

She stood up, grabbed Dawson's glass of water, and threw it in Pacey's face. "You're an arrogant jerk and a pig, Pacey," she said before she stormed off.

Pacey sat there in shocked silence, but that was soon broken by Dawson's laughter. Pacey couldn't believe what Jen had just done—right there in the restaurant for everyone to see!

He glared at Dawson. Why was he laughing?

"Guess you were on the wrong track there," Dawson said, smiling. "Don't drown now! You haven't finished the lifesaving class yet!" He laughed some more at his own joke as Pacey took a napkin and dried his face.

Pacey crumpled the napkin and stood up to leave. He tossed the napkin in Dawson's laughing face, then noisily shoved his chair in. "Good to see you, pal," he spat. "Not!"

He didn't care that he was still hungry and hadn't ordered. Now that Jen had made a fool out of him, he didn't want to hang around the Icehouse for another minute.

"You're popular today," Joey said to Dawson as she wiped up the table.

Dawson brushed the last tears of laughter from his eyes. "Yeah, well, maybe the heat's getting to everyone," he said. He hadn't meant to laugh at Pacey, but it was preposterous of him to think that Jen liked him. Completely preposterous. Right?

"It's not that hot out," Joey countered. She pulled out her order pad. "What are you going to have?"

"With all the excitement, I haven't decided yet," Dawson said.

"Take your time," Joey said cheerfully.

Dawson eyed her curiously. "Why are you in such a good mood today?"

Joey eagerly sat down. "I had the most amazing date last night," she said excitedly.

"Oh, that's right," Dawson said flatly. "I hope he didn't wear those Hawaiian shorts."

Joey looked at Dawson in surprise. "I can share these things with you, can't I?"

"Sure," Dawson said without much enthusiasm. "Go right ahead."

"I mean," Joey said, "how many hours of Jen interactions did I have to sit through?"

Dawson gave her a sheepish grin. "You're right," he admitted. "How was your date?" he asked, giving her his full attention.

"It was phenomenal," Joey said. Dawson could see Bodie eyeing her from the other side of the restaurant. "Three-minute break!" Joey called to him.

"First, Jeremy picked me up and gave me a dozen roses," she began. "Then we went to see *The Cop Who Couldn't Cry.*"

"Ick," Dawson interrupted.

"I wanted to see it," Joey continued. "But it *was* terrible. Anyway, he had asked Bess what my favorite snack was."

"Milk Duds," Dawson stated.

"No!" Joey said, wounded. "Sno-Caps."

"Oh, right," Dawson said. "Continue."

"So he surprised me with the Sno-Caps."

Dawson suddenly decided that he didn't want to hear this. Picturing Joey on a date was starting to upset his stomach. "Sounds like fun. You know, I don't think I'm going to order anything. I'm not hungry anymore." He stood up to go.

"But I'm not finished!" Joey protested.

Dawson sat back down. He hoped she would hurry up and finish this story.

"So the funny thing was that Clarissa's pet started to beep in the middle of the movie, and we started having a laughing fit because it was right in the middle of the most dramatic scene. So we left."

Dawson stood up again. "That's funny."

Joey pushed him back down in his seat. "I'm still not done. It turned out that Jeremy had already seen the movie anyway, but he sat through it again because I really wanted to see it."

Dawson laughed. This guy sounded like a sap case. "That's so corny! What a dork!"

"Hey!" Joey yelled, hurt. "He is not a dork! He is charming, funny, and adorable, and he's a great date. The best date I've ever had in my life!" She ripped the menu out of Dawson's hand. "If you're not going to order, you can't sit at a table," she snapped, then stomped over to the bar.

Dawson put his head in his hands. Great. Just great. Pacey was mad at him. Jen could barely say a sentence to him. And now Joey would probably never talk to him again.

Chapter 14

Joey couldn't decide which bathing suit to wear. She only had two that she felt were decent. The others were old and ragged, and she had quickly grown out of them.

She'd been wearing the red one when Jeremy met her, but it was her favorite, and the newest. Her other option wasn't nearly as exciting: it was navy blue and not cut as high on the legs.

She decided she had no choice but to go with the red one. She pulled on the suit, then put on shorts and a T-shirt. Glancing out the window, Joey could see that the sky was clear, and it looked like this was going to be a beautiful day.

She jumped when she heard a knock at the front door. She glanced at the clock. That was probably Jeremy! Bess and Bodie were at the Icehouse with the baby, so she had to answer the door herself.

After checking her appearance in the mirror, she calmly walked to the door. Though she was bursting with excitement, she knew it wouldn't be cool to appear too eager. But when she pulled the door open, all serenity left her.

"Hey!" Jeremy said, smiling his huge smile. Joey loved the way the corners of his mouth curved up and the way his eyes crinkled when he smiled. She wondered if he noticed little things like that about her, too.

"Hi." Joey returned his greeting and wide smile. "I'm ready," she said, grabbing her bag and stepping out the front door. She noticed that he was wearing the same Hawaiian shorts he'd had on the day before. That made her feel better about wearing the red bathing suit. But today Jeremy also wore a bright red retro bowling shirt. The word "Bird" was stitched over the pocket.

"Is that your nickname?" Joey asked, playfully pointing at his chest.

"No," Jeremy answered, shaking his head. "It's the nickname of my favorite jazz musician, Charlie Parker. I saw this shirt in an antique clothing store and I just had to have it. It called out to me."

"That's cool," Joey said. "That you like jazz. I don't know much about it, but my mother used to listen to jazz all the time. She had all these Ella Fitzgerald and Louis Armstrong records."

"The true greats," Jeremy said. "Next time I come to Capeside, I'll bring my sax."

So he plays the saxophone, Joey thought. She was looking forward to finding out more about him. At the movies the other night, they hadn't had a chance to talk too much, and there was so much she wanted to know about him.

Jeremy was carrying a cooler and a duffel bag. He held up the cooler for Joey to see. "I packed us some lunch—stopped at the deli. Today's menu features chicken salad or roast beef sandwiches and potato chips."

"No Sno-Caps?" Joey teased.

"Ah, yes," Jeremy said, smiling. "The roast beef is actually encrusted with Sno-Caps, making for a delicate blend of flavors."

"Yum!" Joey exclaimed.

Jeremy threw the strap of the duffel bag over his shoulder, so he would have a free hand. He reached for Joey's hand and took it in his. Joey liked the way his hand felt around hers. It was warm and cozy and strong. Not sweaty and clammy like some boys' hands.

Walking down the street with Jeremy, Joey felt special. He made her feel interesting and beautiful and fun.

When they reached the beach, they spread out a blanket. Jeremy pulled a Frisbee and a paddleball set out of the duffel bag. "So we won't get bored staring into each other's eyes," he said.

Joey laughed, but she thought that she would be content to stare at him all day.

"How's Howard?" Jeremy asked as he sat down.

"Still alive and kicking," Joey answered, as she sank down on the blanket. "Thanks to you," she added.

They stretched out side by side on the blanket and began to talk. Joey was struck by how easy the conversation was. She never had to rack her brain to think of something to say. There was never an awkward pause or dull lull.

They talked about their schools and their families. Joey told him the truth about her dad, and she was relieved that Jeremy didn't seem at all fazed.

"My family is far from perfect, too," he assured her. He told her that he liked to play soccer and that he loved to travel. He said it was his dream to visit all seven continents.

Joey imagined jetting off to Paris with Jeremy. Or going on safari in Africa to photograph beautiful and unusual animals. Or holding him close on a secluded iceberg somewhere near Antarctica. Or just sitting on the beach in Capeside for many summers to come.

Joey felt the heat beat down on her. Today was already a scorcher, but she couldn't tell if it was the sun or being close to Jeremy that made her feel hot. She decided to go for a swim before she started to sweat. She didn't think perspiration would be very appealing, so she challenged Jeremy to race her to the water.

It was a perfect day for a swim. The sun was bright. The water was calm. The beach was quiet, for a Sunday. She laughed all the way to the cooling blue water. And right then she was happier than she'd ever been before in her life.

Dawson slowly circled the beach blanket, ending with a close-up of Sheila. "Tell me about Australia," he said.

He sat down next to her on the blanket under the

huge beach umbrella. Dawson preferred to sit right under the scorching summer sun, but the umbrella had to be there to protect the babies.

Sheila adjusted the strap on her blue tie-dyed bikini. "What do you want to know?" she asked.

"I don't know," Dawson said, carefully steadying the camera, slightly distracted by her beautiful figure. Since Sheila had said she was camera-shy, Dawson hadn't told her about his news story opportunity. He figured he'd wait until the end of the day to inform her. That way she'd be more natural in front of the camera as he filmed her. Dawson's heart started to beat a little faster. He was happy that he felt something for her. "Tell me about your life there," Dawson probed. "Do you miss it?"

Sheila's expression grew sad. "I miss some things," she answered vaguely, "but other things I don't miss at all."

How mysterious, Dawson thought. She must have some deep, dark secrets. But he could tell she didn't want to be pressed about the things she didn't miss. "Tell me about the things you miss," he encouraged.

Sheila's expression grew wistful. "I miss my friends. I miss meat pies. I miss scuba diving at the reef, seeing all the colorful amazing fish." Her expression grew tender at the memories.

"Did you come to the States alone?" he asked.

Sheila nodded.

"Wow," Dawson said. "That's amazing."

Sheila shrugged. "Aussies are big travelers. Sometimes we go away just to think. We call that a walkabout. I guess I'm kind of on a walkabout for a while."

"What about Boston?" Dawson continued.

"Boston?" Sheila repeated, puzzled.

"Do you miss Boston? That's where you came first, right?"

"Oh, yeah, Boston," Sheila said vaguely. "Actually, I like it better here in Capeside."

Dawson could tell that Sheila wanted to change the subject. "I'll take some beach background shots," he told her, turning the camera away.

Things were going well so far, Dawson mused. He didn't want to screw it up by putting Sheila on the spot, asking her prying questions. But he couldn't help wondering how tough it must be for a teenager to go abroad alone. It sounded kind of cool, but kind of lonely, too.

Dawson pushed questions about Sheila's past out of his mind and concentrated on the setting. He had gotten some great shots already. He had arrived at the Barclays' just in time this morning. Sheila was awake, but the babies weren't. They had shared some juice until Sheila heard the first cry of the morning. After Sheila had changed and fed the twins, they came to the beach, and what a perfect day it was for it. Dawson panned the ocean, the sand, the sky, Joey . . . *Joey?* Dawson stopped panning his camera. A familiar brown-haired girl in a red bathing suit was running to a blanket, hand in hand with a boy. He would have recognized those Hawaiian shorts anywhere. It was Joey, with that guy, Jeremy.

Dawson zoomed in on Joey and Jeremy as they collapsed on the blanket, giggling. Then—Dawson couldn't believe his eyes—they kissed. *Really* kissed. Right there on the beach!

"Oh, my God!" Dawson said, his camera transfixed on the frolicking young couple. "I can't believe them! Right in the middle of a public beach!"

"Who? What?" Sheila asked excitedly.

Dawson pointed toward Joey and Jeremy. "Over there. It's disgusting!"

"Let me see." Sheila eagerly peered through Dawson's lens. "Aw, they're perfectly sweet! Wait—isn't that the girl who's in all your movies?"

"Yes," Dawson said, taking the camera back and focusing in on them. "I don't know about this guy. . . ."

Sheila started to laugh.

"What's so funny?" Dawson asked.

"It's so obvious, Dawson," Sheila said. "You're annoyed because you're completely into her. You're *jealous*."

Dawson gasped. "I—I . . . That's not true!" He didn't know what to say. But he did feel a familiar pang in his chest.

But he had his sights on Sheila! Didn't she see that? How could she have noticed all this stuff between him and Joey without seeing that he was there, right in front of her, dying to get to know her?

There was only one way she'd get it, Dawson thought. He put down the camera, impulsively grabbed Sheila by the shoulders, and planted a huge kiss on her lips.

When he pulled back, Dawson sighed. Nothing. It was about as exciting as kissing Pacey, he thought. It wasn't like kissing Joey at all. He longed for that feeling again. Why wasn't that chemistry there with Sheila?

Sheila giggled. "Nice try, Dawson. But I still think you two make a darling couple."

Dawson started to think that maybe Sheila was right.

Chapter 15

On Sunday morning Pacey didn't show up to walk Jen to class. Not that she expected him to. After all, she had thrown a glass of water in his face. But even though Jen was mad at him, she felt that something was missing. No latte. No Pacey.

She sighed. Just when she thought she had a new friend, things had started to get ugly. Was it her fault? Had she overreacted?

When she arrived at class, Pacey was already there, chatting up a few girls. He glanced at Jen briefly, but coldly turned away when she came to join the group.

The class snapped to attention when Tim strode over. "Everyone into the pool for laps," he ordered.

Jen groaned inwardly. The laps were tiring, and this morning she hadn't had her coffee. But she understood the importance of becoming a strong swimmer to save lives. Apparently Pacey didn't feel the same way.

While the trainees dutifully swam their laps, Tim sat in a chair and leafed through a magazine. Thanks to Pacey, Jen figured he didn't want to leave the class alone anymore while they were swimming.

But leave it to Pacey to continue to goof off. While Tim flipped through his magazine, Pacey swam one lap to everyone else's two. Then, when people finished and climbed out of the pool, Pacey climbed out, too, after swimming only half as many laps as everyone else.

Jen shot him a dirty look. Pacey didn't belong in this class. Tim's approach might be harsh and comical, but he was right: lifesaving was an important skill, and there was no room for slacking off and goofing around. Tim was giving them essential job training, and his military manner was effective in making everyone pay attention and take the class seriously. Everyone except for Pacey.

After they finished their laps, Tim lectured them about rescue skills, such as how to hold and tow a drowning swimmer. Tim said that these were among the most important skills they would learn in class and that he would test them repeatedly.

But while Tim was lecturing and demonstrating, Jen could see that Pacey's eyes were closing behind his sunglasses. He wasn't paying attention to a bit of what Tim said.

"If a person is in distress," Tim explained, "he or she is in a panic. It is very important that you don't worsen the situation. The first thing you need to do when saving a person in distress is to calm the person down.

"Always, *always* take a life buoy or flotation device with you when saving someone," Tim continued emphatically. Tim couldn't stress the importance of these basics enough. Jen wrote everything down. She noticed that Pacey didn't even have a pen.

"Never, ever grab the person during a rescue," Tim went on.

One of the guys raised his hand. "But in movies and stuff, you always see the lifeguard swimming out, grabbing the victim, and towing him in. Is that wrong?" he asked uncertainly.

Tim chuckled. "One thing I want you all to know," Tim said, "is that lifeguarding on television and in the movies is entirely fake. Those people are actors and actresses. They are not in real-life situations."

Tim glanced at each class member. "Understand? Don't ever, ever use television or movies as your reference point for lifeguarding.

"When you approach a frightened victim, he may be thrashing around." Tim moved his arms wildly about to illustrate the point. "If you come too close to him, he can harm you, too, and all of your lifesaving efforts will be useless."

Tim's expression grew serious. "I have seen five- and six-year-olds, one-third the size of an adult nearly choke a lifesaver to death because the lifeguard acted in the wrong manner. And of course if a big guy like me was in a panic, he would drown you almost instantly."

Tim's voice grew urgent. "*Always* bring the victim

in with a life preserver. Hand him the buoy. Never try to grab him."

This sounded like serious stuff, Jen thought. She heard a light snore come from her right side. Half the class turned to look.

Pacey was dozing. The girl next to him elbowed him, and he snapped awake. He tried to act casual, but Jen could see that Tim had noticed.

Tim ignored Pacey for the moment, but Jen suspected that he was writing himself a mental note about Pacey. And he wasn't writing it in pencil. He was carving it in stone.

Pacey was back at the pool right after lunch, performing all sorts of stupid-human tricks and showing off in the water. He was doing dumb daredevil dives, too, in the shallow end of the pool The other girls seemed to be growing tired of his one-man show, and Jen simply couldn't take it anymore.

If he wanted to crack his head on the shallow end of the pool, that was his own problem, Jen thought. But if he didn't know what to do in a lifesaving situation because he hadn't paid attention in class, that was another case altogether. He could cause someone else to die.

But that was, of course, if Pacey actually became a lifeguard. At this point, Jen figured he would never pass the exam.

"You know, Pacey, you should stop goofing around and pay attention in class," Jen said, unable to hold her tongue any longer. "You're never going to pass the exam at this rate."

Pacey shot her a cold stare. "What is it with

you?" he asked angrily. "I think you made your point yesterday that you're not jealous. So what is your problem? Why are you always on my back?"

"Because I like you Pacey," Jen said, "and I don't want to see you make any more dumb mistakes."

"Well, thanks for your concern," Pacey said sarcastically. "But I already have one mother."

Then he took a running leap and turned a somersault into the pool, making a huge splash that drenched Jen.

How obnoxious can you get? Jen thought.

Where Pacey was concerned, it seemed there was no limit.

Dawson put his camera down and lay on the beach blanket that he had moved out of the umbrella's shadow. The sun shone down on him like a huge interrogation light. What did he feel for Joey? It was all too confusing.

She had been his best friend all his life. Earlier he'd never thought of her as a girlfriend.

Then things had changed. He and Joey had kissed a few times. At first he didn't think the kisses meant anything. But the memories had lingered. And then romantic thoughts of Joey had slowly crept into his mind.

Now he had seen another side of Joey. How attractive she was to other guys. How her chestnut-brown hair shone in the sun, how cute and shy her smile was, how just a touch of lipstick accentuated her lips. Dawson wanted to kiss them again.

But could friends be lovers? Wouldn't it make

sense, Dawson thought, for the love of your life to be your best friend?

And what about Sheila? Was there any hope of a spark developing there? Dawson knew the answer was no.

Sheila stirred and started to pack a bag. "I think the babies have gotten more than enough sun," she said.

That reminded Dawson—he hadn't told her about the news story yet. "Hey!" he said, sitting up excitedly. "I guess I'll tell you now."

"Tell me what?"

"My mother is an anchorperson for the local news station. She happens to be doing a piece on teens and their summer jobs."

Sheila's eyes widened.

Dawson smiled at Sheila's expression of surprise. He went on. "So she thinks you would be the perfect candidate for the piece. She said it would give her series the international flair it needs. Isn't that great? You roll into Capeside as a nanny, and now you'll end up a television star!"

Sheila froze.

"I know," Dawson said. "Isn't it amazing? And she said I could do the piece. I could use the footage from today."

"But you said it was for practice only!" Sheila said. "You lied! How could you do this to me?"

"No!" Dawson assured her. "It *was* for practice. It's just a coincidence that my mom has this story going on. I just thought I could—"

"No," Sheila said abruptly, her face red. "No, you can't. I won't do it. This project is over as of *now*."

She quickly gathered her belongings, slung her tote-bag over her shoulder, and picked up the twin's.

"But—" Dawson protested.

Sheila hurried away across the sand.

He couldn't believe it. He started to chase after Sheila. "Wait!" he called. "There's nothing to be scared of! You looked great while I was taping you! You look terrific! You were completely natural!"

But Sheila didn't turn back.

Dawson stopped. He stood on the beach watching her retreating figure. "That's why I waited to tell you," he finished quietly.

He sank down onto the hot sand, defeated. Pacey was mad at him. Jen hadn't been able to have a conversation with him in weeks. He'd ruined any relationship he might have had with Joey. And now his only remaining friend was furious with him.

How had his life become such a mess?

Chapter 16

Dawson carried his equipment into his room and stretched out on his bed. How had today ended up such a disaster?

First he couldn't get his mind off seeing Joey kiss that guy. He was plagued by images of her, lip-locked with Mr. Loud Shorts.

Then Sheila had gone psycho on him. For the world of him, Dawson couldn't understand her re-action. Was she really *that* shy? Or was it something else?

Already his summer was turning out to be one enormous bummer, like some high-budget film disaster with an overpriced all-star cast. See how one teen single-handedly ticks off every woman in town! Watch with amazement at how he doesn't go on one single date for the rest of his life! Gasp in horror at the dark, disgusting boredom oozing out of every facet of his life. Coming to a theater near you. And hopelessly rated G.

Dawson heard the front door open and shut. That had to be his dad. Maybe he'd talk to him. His father always seemed to be able to make sense out of things.

Dawson walked down the stairs and into the kitchen, where he found his father grabbing a soda from the fridge. "Hey, Dad," Dawson said.

"Dawson," Mr. Leery answered. "I thought you'd be out enjoying this fabulous day."

"I was," Dawson answered. "And it's not that fabulous a day. More like the total opposite."

Dawson's dad regarded him curiously, and sat down at the kitchen table. "Something happen?"

Dawson pulled out a chair and sat across from his father. "Dad," he asked, "have you ever liked more than one girl at the same time?"

His father laughed. "When I was your age, it was more a question of did a girl exist that I *didn't* like."

Dawson let out a heavy breath. "I mean, I just can't get my feelings straight. If Jen wanted me, I'd take her back in a second. But then, I don't know, I think Joey and I could have something special. And then there's Sheila. . . . She's so wonderful, but it just doesn't feel right." He paused thoughtfully. "I guess it doesn't make any difference, though, because they all hate me."

Mr. Leery took a sip of soda, his expression one of fond remembrance. "It's called hormones. You're full of them now. They creep into your bloodstream and your brain and mix everything up."

Dawson was still unsettled. What bothered him

the most was that crazy kiss. The Joey kiss on the beach. With a total stranger. He wondered if Joey thought Mr. Fancy Pants kissed better than he did.

"Dad," Dawson asked carefully, "do you think it's possible for best friends to be lovers?"

"Absolutely," Mr. Leery answered unhaltingly. "Your mother is the best friend I've ever had. *Ever.*"

Dawson nodded thoughtfully.

Mr. Leery looked at him seriously. "Listen to your heart, Dawson. Then go for it."

"Thanks, Dad," Dawson said. He nodded, lost in thought. Then he rose and walked out the back door to stare out across the creek. He'd been acting like a jerk to Joey lately. And he didn't blame her if she was crazy about this new guy. But Dawson wouldn't step aside without a fight.

And what was he going to do about Sheila? Dawson realized that he'd been desperately trying to start a romance with her in a sad attempt to run away from his true feelings. But Sheila'd had it right all along. And he wanted to have her as a friend.

But first things first. He was going to call Joey and apologize for the way he'd acted at the Icehouse. Even if he had missed his chance with her, Dawson thought their friendship was too important to let go of. Maybe they could spend the day together tomorrow, like old times.

He walked back into the house to call her.

When Joey got home, she listened to the message tape on her answering machine: "Hey, Joey, it's Dawson. Sorry about what I said yesterday. I didn't mean it. I was wondering if you wanted to go on a bike ride or something tomorrow morning. Give me a call."

Dawson sounded pretty normal, Joey thought. She was happy that he'd apologized. She hadn't been able to spend any quality time with him in the past two days because she had been so busy with Jeremy. She liked the idea of getting together with Dawson and doing something fun.

She called him back and left a message: "See you at eight tomorrow morning. It's supposed to be good biking weather."

She'd had an amazing time at the beach with Jeremy that day. They hadn't even ended up playing Frisbee or paddleball. They swam and shared lunch and a few kisses, but they spent most of the day talking, and Joey discovered so many wonderful things about him.

Tonight Jeremy was going to take her to dinner at Romano's, a fancy restaurant where Joey had eaten only once before. She sat on the couch and closed her eyes, picturing his adorable smile and handsome face.

Bess came in the front door just then, holding a bawling Alexander.

All images of romance instantly dissolved. "Hey," Joey greeted her sister.

"Hey," Bess said back. "You looked as if you were in outer space."

Joey giggled. "Kind of."

Bodie strolled into the house, holding out the baby's formula. "You left this in the hot car," he said to Bess, sounding annoyed.

"Oh," Bess answered. "Thanks for bringing it in."

Bodie's face was hard. "Where is your head lately? You made a bazillion accounting errors at the restaurant today. You leave the baby's stuff all over town. I'm surprised we still have him, and that you haven't left him behind somewhere!"

Bess put the baby on the couch next to Joey. She turned on Bodie, hands planted defiantly on her hips. "Well, if you were the one getting up nights to feed him, you'd be forgetful, too. Sometimes you seem to forget *that*."

Joey could tell that they were gearing up for a big-league blowup. It was so depressing to watch them fight after she'd had such a great day.

Bodie slammed the baby's bottle down on the coffee table. "I've been working quadruple overtime to make sure that this child is provided for! Don't tell me I don't contribute!" Then he turned to Joey. "And look at this house! It's a mess! Joey, you were off today. Couldn't you at least have put the dishes in the dishwasher?"

Joey was angry that he put her in the middle of this. "Hey!" she said. "No one told you two to have a baby. Don't blame me if the responsibility is too much for you in your warped game of playing house!"

"You don't know anything about responsibility," Bess cut in. "You're conveniently never around to understand how hard it is! I'm bringing you up, too. You *could* help out more around here."

Joey couldn't believe it. They were ganging up on her. What had she done to deserve this? "You are not bringing me up!" Joey lashed out. *"Mom* brought me up. Don't you dare take the credit! *You* will never be Mom."

The room fell silent. Bodie looked away. Bess stood as if she had been slapped in the face.

Then the baby started to cry again. Bess picked him up and cradled him in her arms, still looking hurt.

Joey got up and ran out the front door, slamming it hard behind her. She had to get out. She had to get away.

She ran hard and fast, as fast as she could, away from her family, past and present.

Tim marched into the pool area and announced, "No more lecturing for the rest of the day. This afternoon you will learn by example. This morning I talked about what to do in a rescue situation. Now we'll do some rescue practices in the pool."

Pacey was psyched. Finally they'd get to the good stuff and spend more time in the water and less time sitting on their butts.

"I'm going to play the victim each time," Tim said, pulling off his T-shirt and sunglasses but leaving his whistle around his neck. When I call you, I want you to follow all of the correct procedures to rescue me."

Tim jumped into the pool and sized up the group. "Witter," he said. "I will pretend to be a distressed swimmer. I want you to rescue me."

Pacey nodded. This should be easy enough, he thought.

Tim submerged himself. He swam a few laps.

Then he stopped and treaded water for a few seconds.

Pacey took that as his sign, and he leaped into the water.

Tim immediately blew his whistle. "What was wrong with that, folks?" he asked the class.

Pacey stood in the pool, confused. He hadn't even started to save Tim. How could he be doing something wrong already?

One of the twins—Pacey wasn't sure if it was Mindy or Mallory—raised her hand. "You didn't show any sign of distress," she pointed out, then giggled. "He went running in there for no reason."

"Exactly," Tim confirmed. "Pacey here just attacked a confident swimmer who was minding his own business."

The entire class laughed at him then. Pacey steamed up inside. He'd like to see any of these other clowns do better.

Tim looked Pacey right in the eye. "Okay, now," he said. "We're going to try this again. Are you ready this time?" he challenged.

"Yes," Pacey asserted. "I'm ready."

Tim wouldn't back off. "Are you sure?"

Pacey gritted his teeth and hopped out of the pool. "Yes, I'm sure," he responded.

"Then sit in the lifeguard chair," Tim said. "Don't hover at the edge of the pool. That's unrealistic."

Pacey walked over to the tall chair and started to climb the ladder. Just when he turned his back, he heard a thrashing in the water. He figured Tim was just swimming around, but when he sat in the chair, all eyes of the class were staring at him.

Tim blew the whistle again. "What are you, deaf?" he asked. "I'd be dead by now, if I waited for you."

"I—I had my back turned! That wasn't fair!" Pacey protested.

"That was more than fair," Tim corrected. He turned to the class. "Why was that fair?" he asked the group.

One guy raised his hand. "If he is the lifeguard on duty, he should never have his back turned. He should always be alert and scanning the area. Also, he should have acted as soon as he heard the splashing, but he didn't even turn around."

"Correct," Tim said. "Class, what lifeguard bylaw applies to what we have just seen?"

"A lifeguard is always prepared," the class chorused.

"Exactly," Tim said.

Pacey sat in the chair, turning a deep shade of red. Why was Tim picking on him? This was totally unfair.

"Now," Tim said to Pacey, "I'll give you one more chance. Are you ready?"

"Yeah," Pacey mumbled, embarrassed.

"I can't hear you!" Tim bellowed.

"Yes," Pacey said louder. He saw his classmates whispering and snickering. And Jen's sanctimonious glare seemed stuck on him. He'd show them all this time. They'd see a rescue that would make David Hasselhoff jealous.

"Okay, then," Tim said. He blew his whistle. "Let's go."

Tim swam a few lazy laps. Pacey didn't take his

eyes off him. Tim stopped and treaded water. Pacey sat stone-still in the chair. He wasn't falling for that again. Tim swam around a little bit more, and all eyes were glued to him as the trainees watched for signs of distress.

Finally Tim went under. Pacey watched him. He didn't panic. He saw him swimming underwater. When Tim came up, he seemed normal. He was.

Tim went under a second time, but this time he resurfaced quickly and began flailing his arms and kicking his legs in a panic.

Pacey acted immediately.

Instantly he climbed down from the lifeguard chair, dived into the water, swam right to Tim, and threw his arms around him.

Which tow should I use? Pacey searched his mind. There was the one where you dragged the victim from behind. But wasn't that for a swimmer with a spinal injury? Or not?

Pacey found it hard to concentrate with Tim thrashing around. He tried to pull him, but the next thing he knew, Tim had him in a stranglehold, and he wouldn't let go. Pacey went under because of the pressure of Tim grabbing on to him.

Then Pacey started to panic. Was Tim trying to drown him, right there in front of the class? He knew the instructor had it in for him, but was he crazy enough to kill him? Did he hate Pacey that much? Tim was obviously deranged! Why wasn't anyone trying to help?

Pacey started to yell, "Help me! Help!"

Finally Tim released his grip. Pacey kicked and splashed his way to the edge of the pool. Gasping and coughing, he pulled himself out of the water. Pacey glared at Tim, who was laughing. What kind of a maniac was this guy?

"Congratulations, Witter," Tim said. "You killed us both."

The entire class burst into laughter.

"*You* killed us both," Pacey said defensively. "You were strangling me!"

Tim waded over to the edge of the pool and propped his elbows on the concrete. "No, Pacey," he said quietly. "*You* killed us. You had no idea what you were doing, did you?"

Pacey stared at Tim in guilty silence. Without saying anything, he grabbed a towel and wrapped it around his shoulders. The whole class stared at him, and this time they weren't laughing.

Pacey wanted to dive into the water and never come up.

"If this had been a real situation," Tim said, "there would have been two victims."

Pacey swallowed hard and looked at the ground. When was this torture going to end?

"Ladies and gentlemen, I do want you to know that Pacey *did* do a good job," Tim said lightly. "He did a great job, as a matter of fact, of showing you all precisely how *not* to act in a lifesaving situation.

"Thank you, Pacey," Tim said.

Pacey didn't even look at him. He slunk over to the group and sat down on the hot concrete.

"Now who is going to show us how a real lifeguard should act?" Tim asked. "Who will be my next victim? Or savior?"

Tim scanned the worried faces in the crowd.

Pacey felt self-satisfied. No one else wanted to be made an example of.

Tim's eyes fell on Jen. "Miss Lindley? How about you?"

Jen stood up immediately. "Yes, sir," she answered.

Pacey felt even worse. That was all he needed now—to have Jen, of all people, show him up. He hoped she would fail. For once, Pacey thought, let someone else feel as embarrassed as I do.

Jen walked to the lifeguard chair and carefully watched Tim as he swam. She continued to keep her eye on him as she quickly climbed up the ladder.

She looks so smug in that chair, Pacey thought. Sitting there like she's the queen of lifesaving.

Tim reacted suddenly this time. Seconds after Jen planted herself in the chair, he started to thrash in the water.

Pacey watched as Jen responded immediately.

She grabbed the bright orange life buoy that hung next to her on the chair, then climbed down.

The life buoy! Pacey thought. I forgot about that!

Then Jen jumped into the water and swam rapidly toward Tim.

"Okay, take it easy," Jen said soothingly. "Grab the life buoy. Hold on to the life preserver and everything will be okay."

Tim advanced toward Jen in a panic, but Jen thrust the buoy toward him, while backing slightly away. Tim grabbed the buoy, and with the situation totally under control, Jen towed him to the edge of the pool.

Tim blew his whistle. "Excellent!" he said. "Class, I want you to give Jen a round of applause. She did everything perfectly."

Pacey clapped reluctantly along with the class. What a show-off she was, he thought. Little Miss Can't-Be-Wrong.

"Now, Jen," Tim said. "For bonus points: If I'd been unconscious, what would you have done when you got me on land?"

Jen wrinkled her forehead in concentration. Pacey smirked. He didn't think they had learned this yet. Or had they? He wanted to see Little Miss Can't-Be-Wrong get this one right.

"I would check the pulse, then check for breathing," Jen answered, nodding. "Then I would give you artificial respiration, or CPR, depending on what the situation called for."

"Perfect, once again," Tim said. "Class, I want you to remember Jen's actions today. She took absolutely correct lifesaving precautions."

She could use an absolutely correct enema, Pacey thought later that afternoon as he neared his house and tried to wipe the afternoon out of his mind. He was glad to be out of his misery, for today, at least. Tomorrow was sure to be another story.

He didn't know how much more he could take. Of lifesaving or of Jen.

Chapter 17

Joey went for a long, solitary walk on the beach and returned to the house only when she was sure that Bess and Bodie would be at the restaurant. She had to get ready for her date tonight and she wanted to dress in peace.

She had cooled down from the argument, but she was still mad at how Bess and Bodie always put her in the middle of their problems. They had never acted like that before the baby was born. Sure, her nephew was adorable, and they all loved him. But he had no idea how much trouble he caused in the family.

Joey felt that she needed a vacation. She needed to get away from Bess and Bodie and the baby. The house was too small for the four of them.

She also needed a vacation from boring old Capeside. She wanted to go somewhere else—anywhere else. Somewhere far away where she had no family, no job, and no school.

Joey turned her thoughts away from her family strife and back to her date. Thank God for Jeremy, she thought. Without him the summer would be nothing but working, baby-sitting, and fighting.

When she was with Jeremy, all of that seemed far away and insignificant. She sure hoped the summer would pass slowly. She didn't know what she would do when it was over and Jeremy had to go back to New Hampshire. She didn't even want to think about it.

Maybe she could earn enough money this summer to pay him a few visits in New Hampshire in the fall. That would certainly be a worthwhile and well-deserved getaway vacation.

She wondered what life was like for Jeremy in New Hampshire. He had said his town wasn't that different from Capeside. Joey laughed at the thought. She couldn't imagine another place just as dull. It had to be more exciting. After all, Jeremy lived there.

Joey wanted to dress up for tonight. She looked in her closet and moved things aside until she found the perfect outfit—a short, lightweight powder-blue dress. It was from last summer, but it was still in style. It would be cool enough for a hot summer night and sexy enough for a romantic dinner at Romano's.

She sprayed a bit of perfume on her neck and winced as the cool spray hit her. She wasn't used to wearing perfume, but she wanted to smell nice. Then she rummaged in her jewelry box for the perfect baubles. She found them: tiny, elegant pearl earrings and a delicate pearl necklace.

She completed the outfit with strappy sandals. Looking at herself in the mirror, Joey smiled. She glanced at the clock. She was to meet Jeremy tonight at Romano's, but it was still too early to go.

She picked up Howard and played with him for a little while, just to kill time. She thought about how Jeremy had taught her everything she needed to know about caring for Howard: how to feed him, clean him, give him medicine, put him to bed, discipline him. She now knew what to do in any beeping situation.

Joey examined the pink egg and grinned. When Clarissa came back from her family vacation, Joey would have to thank her. Who would have thought that Howard would bring her Jeremy—and the romance of a lifetime!

The Leery household was quiet except for the clinking of silverware on china as Dawson and his parents sat around the kitchen table. Darkness had fallen, and moonlight peeked in through the windows.

"How's your documentary coming along?" Dawson's mother asked him as she passed the asparagus.

Dawson stopped chewing his chicken. "Um," he stalled with his mouth full. Should he tell his mother that the project was a bust? Or should he talk to Sheila and find out what the problem was?

The latter sounded like the better idea to Dawson. He didn't want to give up on the project just yet.

Before he let Mom down, he would see if he could calm Sheila down.

"It's going to be great," Dawson said. "I got some terrific shots at the Barclay house in this morning and at the beach this afternoon."

Mrs. Leery beamed. "That's great, Dawson. I'm so proud of you for pursuing this. With your enthusiasm and talent, I'm sure my producers will take your piece."

If there is a piece, Dawson thought glumly.

"Just remember to thank the Academy *and* us when you get your Oscar, son," Mr. Leery joked.

"Maybe one day we can work as a team," Mrs. Leery added. "A mother-and-son investigative reporting team!"

The more excited his mother became, the more uncomfortable Dawson grew. He didn't want to disappoint her. He had to find some way to get Sheila to change her mind.

Dawson speared another piece of chicken. Looking up at his mom, he was suddenly struck with an idea. Maybe, just maybe, if he used some of the professional editing equipment at the station, he could put together a brief clip to show to Sheila, to clarify for her what he was doing, and especially to reveal how wonderfully she came off on camera. With the high-tech stuff they used at the station, Dawson was sure he could put together a piece that would wow her.

"I was wondering," Dawson said between bites, "if I could use some of the station's editing equipment."

Mrs. Leery looked at Dawson in surprise. "Don't tell me you're finished already?"

"No," Dawson admitted, "but I want to put together a sample film to surprise Sheila—just to give her a teaser of what's to come."

Mrs. Leery nodded. "I don't see a problem with that," she said. "But it has to be early in the morning, before the editors get in. I wouldn't want you to interfere with their work."

"Okay," Dawson agreed. "I'll go with you to the station early tomorrow, then."

"Great," Mr. Leery added. "Tomorrow will be Bring Your Son to Work Day, honey."

Dawson breathed a sigh of relief. This might just work. With a few nifty editing tricks, he might be able to save the documentary—and his friendship with Sheila—after all.

Pacey dribbled the basketball, slamming it into the blacktop as he ran down the court and planted a layup right in the basket.

He stopped, peeled off his shirt, and wiped the sweat from his brow. He'd been at it since he came home from lifesaving class.

He walked over to the grass and collapsed. He always came to the school yard when he needed to think. In the summertime there was never a soul around, so it was quiet enough for him to sort things out.

Plus he could play basketball without his brother harassing him, reminding him he was a loser.

Pacey's head was spinning from the events of the

day. Class had been awful, and when he left the pool, he had been steaming mad.

He was mad at Tim. He was mad at Jen. He was mad at the world. He had been caught napping—literally.

But now that he had cooled off, Pacey was getting that sinking feeling. That feeling that maybe he should be angry with himself.

Once again he was the town screwup. No big surprise, Pacey thought. He wondered why he'd ever thought he could be anything but a big fat failure at everything he pursued. He had earned that loser label for a reason, he figured.

He had to face the facts. He had been goofing off in class. He hadn't been paying attention.

Maybe he wanted to be a lifeguard for the wrong reasons. Saving lives had never really crossed his mind when he pictured himself sitting up in the chair, surrounded by adoring babes.

And Jen was right. He had been acting like a jerk, telling outrageous lies to impress the girls. He had ignored Jen, refusing to see that she was trying to be his friend. Then he had insulted her when his inflated ego had led him to guess wrong about why she was angry.

Now she was furious with him. Everything felt all wrong.

Pacey got up and stepped onto the court once again. He took a foul shot.

Swoosh! He shoots, he scores, Pacey thought. Too bad life wasn't like a basketball court: a place where you could focus on one goal and, with enough practice, you could make the shot. The crowd was there to cheer you on. And if you missed, it didn't hurt so bad. There would always be other shots. Your chances would improve with each toss. You could make up for missing the last shot by sinking the next one.

He wanted another shot with Jen. He didn't want to lose her friendship. He wanted to make things right again.

But to do that, he knew what his first step had to be: he had to apologize.

Romano's wasn't too crowded, and it wasn't too empty. Candles flickered throughout the room, dripping just a touch of wax on the silver holders. Tuxedoed waiters bustled through the restaurant, making sure everything was just so. Joey and Jeremy had ordered lobster—her favorite.

Joey was pleased that her dress had received an approving glance and wide smile from Jeremy when she arrived at the restaurant. He looked great, too, Joey mused, in his clean white shirt and blue blazer. This time Jeremy had presented her with a single white rose. She loved his old-fashioned romantic gestures. They made her glow, and they made her feel beautiful and glamorous—less like a teenage girl, more like a woman.

The whole scene was perfect, Joey thought. The lights were just dim enough. A strolling violinist serenaded a couple in the corner for their anniversary. A full band was setting up for swing dancing. The whole place seemed to have a rosy glow.

Joey sat across from Jeremy, sipping a soda. Jeremy had an especially rosy glow—a sunburn. "You got a lot of sun today," she said, noticing the blush that covered his nose and cheeks.

"Yeah," Jeremy agreed, "but it will probably be all gone by the time I get home tomorrow."

Joey nearly choked on her soda. *"Tomorrow?"*

"Yeah," Jeremy said, his face falling when he noticed Joey's shocked expression. "I was only here for a long weekend. You didn't think—"

"I did," Joey said, half sad, half angry. Visions of a carefree, endless summer of love dissipated instantly. "I thought you were here for the whole season."

Jeremy shook his head sadly. "I don't know what to say. I thought you knew. I guess I assumed . . ." He threw up his hands in frustration. "I don't know what I'm trying to say. I suppose I should have made that more clear."

Yes, Joey thought. He should have made it clear before she got her hopes up about spending the rest of the summer with him. He should have made it clear so she could have been prepared to say goodbye. He should have made it clear before she let herself fall madly in love with him.

"I'm so sorry," Jeremy said. "But we'll keep in touch. I'll call and write, and if I can save enough money, I'll visit."

Joey nodded. "Sure," she said flatly. She knew all of this had to come to an end, but so soon? Had he looked at her as just a weekend romance? Was he the type of guy who had a girl in every port?

Their waiter came by with their lobsters, placing one in front of each of them. Joey glumly stared down at hers. She suddenly didn't feel much like eating.

Jeremy didn't look as if he had an appetite either. He ignored his food and reached across the table for Joey's hand. "I'm sorry for the misunderstanding," he said. "But I want you to know that these few days with you have been the best in my entire life. I've never met a girl like you before, Joey."

Joey thought that Jeremy sounded so earnest. She wanted to believe him. But she also didn't want him to know how deeply hurt she was. "It's no big deal," she said, casually waving a hand. She forced a smile. "About the misunderstanding. I mean, we were just having fun. It had to end sometime, right?"

Jeremy looked as if he was about to say something, but he hesitated. "Would you excuse me for a minute?" he asked. "I'll be right back, I promise," he assured her. "Don't go anywhere."

Joey wondered if she should take this chance to run out the door and never come back. But she thought better of it. She knew that would be immature and foolish. Even though she was upset that he was leaving so soon, she wanted to spend the few last valuable moments with him.

Anyway, she should have known better than to think he'd stay all summer. Life just wasn't supposed to go her way. Some overwhelming higher power was watching her, making sure that every situation would be as difficult for her as possible. Why did she even bother having hopes and dreams?

Joey stared at the flickering candle flame dancing in front of her. She couldn't believe her bad luck.

No sooner had she found her knight in shining armor than he went racing away, back to New Hampshire. How would she ever get through the rest of the summer? How was she going to get through the rest of her life?

How could Jeremy just casually come to Capeside, take her heart, and then leave?

Joey suddenly heard a familiar voice boom through the restaurant. "May I have your attention, ladies and gentlemen."

It was Jeremy. He was standing at the microphone over where the band was setting up. The musicians had stepped aside, and Jeremy stood alone on the stage. Joey felt her face get hot with embarrassment. What was he doing?

"This is dedicated to the one I love," he said sweetly. He looked at Joey with intense eyes. "Joey, someday we'll be together. I'm sorry that it can't be now. But in the meantime, whenever I hear this song, I will think of you. I hope you will do the same. It's called 'Summertime.'" Then a band member handed Jeremy a saxophone. He strapped it on and started to play.

Joey recognized the tune from *Porgy and Bess.* She was touched by Jeremy's gesture, but she was touched for another reason, too. Her mother always played Ella Fitzgerald's jazzy version of the song when she was in a good mood. The memory brought tears to Joey's eyes.

Jeremy walked right over to their table as he wailed on the saxophone, the smooth notes blending into a swaying melody. He knelt in front of her, his face a mask of passion, his fingers magically moving up and down the instrument's golden throat.

Joey couldn't help but get caught up in the music. He sure was good. She smiled at him appreciatively. He certainly had the golden touch, in music and in romance. She appreciated his attentiveness and his sweet gestures, no matter how brief.

If he was going to leave so soon, at least he was giving her memories. Memories of a summer she would never forget.

Chapter 18

She stepped out of the car, and it sped away. The propellers of the plane whirred in the background. Fog crept up all around her. The mist was cool on her face; she pulled the brim of her hat down.

Jeremy pulled the brim of his hat down, too, and stubbed out the cigarette he'd been smoking. That's funny, Joey thought. I don't remember him smoking. Then again, I've know him for only a few days, Joey reminded herself.

Jeremy took her hand. "Come on," he said, pulling her along. "We're going to miss the plane."

She picked up the small bag sitting on the tarmac. Jeremy lifted his saxophone case. Hand in hand they walked toward the plane.

Finally they were leaving Capeside behind. My dream come true, Joey thought. Jeremy was going to whisk her away somewhere exotic. She couldn't wait.

But Joey stopped in her tracks when she heard a faint voice calling her back. She could barely make it out above the plane engines, but it was there. "Wait!" the voice called.

She turned toward the voice. Appearing out of the fog was Dawson Leery.

"Why are you here, Dawson?" Joey asked. "Don't ruin my departure! Don't ruin my dream! Who asked you to come here?"

Strangely, Dawson was smoking, too. He also wore a hat, its brim pulled down over his eyes. An overcoat hung loosely from his frame. "You expect to dream about one of the greatest movies of all time and not have me appear, sweetheart?" he asked, in a strange voice.

Joey looked frantically from Dawson to Jeremy. "Give me one second," she told Jeremy.

She stormed over to Dawson. "What are you doing here?" she asked. "And when did you start smoking?"

"Old habits die hard," Dawson answered. He drew on the cigarette, then dropped it on the tarmac and stubbed it out with his shoe. "Like you, schweetheart. Like you and me. We're an old habit."

Joey thought Dawson was talking funny. "Stop calling me sweetheart. And when did you pick up the speech impediment? Is that an old habit, too? Or another sign that you've completely lost your mind?"

"Look, sweetheart," Dawson said, unfazed. "All I'm saying is you can leave with him, that stranger who could still turn out to be a psychopath, and hope that the honeymoon won't end." He nodded toward Jeremy, still waiting in the shadows, the fog growing thicker around him. "Or you can stay here with me, the psychopath you know."

"Jeremy's not a psychopath," Joey spat. "But you, on the other hand—"

"Joey darling!" Jeremy's voice called from the fog. "We must go. The plane is leaving. This is our last chance."

Joey began to panic. Something told her she should listen to Dawson. Something told her she should give him a chance. She felt as if a huge invisible magnet was drawing her to him.

Dawson nodded knowingly, but he looked defeated. "He's right, you know. You should go with him. If you stay here, you'll regret it," he said. "Maybe not today, maybe not tomorrow, but soon, and for the rest of your life."

"What about us?" she asked, suddenly overcome with despair at the thought of leaving Dawson.

"We'll always have Capeside," Dawson said. He slowly raised a hand to her face and stroked her chin. "Here's looking at you, kid," he said, then turned and walked away.

Jeremy came over to her, his white suit and hat spotless despite the horrible rainy night. She turned and quickly walked with him to the plane, the engines whirring in the fog.

As her high heels clicked on the tarmac, the decision tore at her heart. A real life with Dawson? Or a fantasy life with Jeremy?

She stopped. She turned.

Impulsively she ran toward the one she knew she must be with.

Joey woke with a start. She sat bolt upright in bed. She had just had the worst nightmare. It was sort of like *Casablanca*. But she was Ilsa, Jeremy was Victor Laszlo, and Dawson was Rick.

In the dream she had to choose between the two boys. In the end, she couldn't believe what had happened: she had chosen Dawson. Thank God it was only a dream.

She thought about the dream as she stretched in her bed. What a dumb dream, she thought, as if she would choose Dawson if she ever had to make that choice in real life. Jeremy could have kicked Dawson's butt all the way from Capeside to Casablanca.

She and Jeremy had had a great farewell date last night. After he played the sax for her, she cheered up and was able to have a good time. The lobster ended up being delicious. They'd even had dessert, and they danced just one slow dance to the big band. It was fun—like nothing she'd ever done with any other boy.

Then Jeremy had walked her home, and once again they shared an earth-shattering kiss. They said their good-byes softly, and she stared after Jeremy as he disappeared into the night, and probably, from her life.

She was able to hold back her tears until she got to her room. She was going to miss him so much.

But still, she felt an uncomfortable tug at her heart from last night's dream. She'd had strong feelings about Dawson once. But when Jeremy came around, those feelings had disappeared.

She'd forgotten what it was like to pine for a boy who saw her as one of the guys. She had forgotten what it was like to get steamed when he chased some other girl. She had almost forgotten all about Dawson.

She threw the covers off. But now, with Jeremy gone, would all of those feelings for Dawson come rushing back?

She sure hoped not. She didn't know if she could stand the torture.

That was when she remembered that she was going to spend the morning with Dawson. Biking.

She figured she'd find out about those feelings soon enough. Right now she had to get going because she knew that Dawson had to work in the afternoon.

Joey threw on shorts and a T-shirt, figuring she'd shower after the bike ride. She pulled on her sneakers and hurried into the kitchen.

She found Bess—exhausted, as usual—feeding the baby. Joey grunted in response to her sister's "Good morning." She hadn't seen her since the big fight the day before. Joey was still a bit steamed about that.

Remembering the fight quickly turned Joey grouchy. Seeing Bess also reminded her of all of the fun times she *wasn't* going to have for the remainder of the summer.

Joey was glad she didn't have to work Mondays. Bodie took over the Icehouse on Mondays, so Bess and Alexander were sure to be sitting around the house all day.

"I'm sorry about yesterday," Bess said, reading Joey's mood. "We didn't mean to pick on you. It's just that sometimes the pressure is too much for us. We shouldn't have taken it out on you."

Joey gulped down a glass of milk, then rinsed the glass and pointedly put it in the drying rack, lest she be reprimanded again for leaving dishes in the sink. She didn't say anything. She didn't feel like talking. Bess could apologize all she wanted, but it wasn't going to change their warped family situation one bit.

"I thought the four of us could do something together today," Bess said tentatively. "You know, like have a family day."

Joey glared at her sister. "I can't play house today. I have plans."

Bess returned the glare.

Joey stomped out the front door, jumped on her bike, and fiercely started to pedal. If Bess and Bodie were going to chastise her for not helping out enough, then they were going to find out what it would be like if she didn't help out at all.

She pedaled around the creek to the Leery house. It was a breezy morning, and Joey started to feel better when she got her adrenaline up.

When she reached Dawson's house, she parked the bike and climbed the ladder into Dawson's room.

"Wake up, sleepyhead!" she called.

But there was no answer. Dawson wasn't there.

She figured that he was probably in the shower.

"Hey, Dawson!" Joey peered around to the bathroom but it was deserted. "Dawson?" she called again.

"Joey?" Mr. Leery called from downstairs. "What brings you here so early in the morning?"

"Dawson," Joey stated. "We were supposed to go bike riding this morning. Where is he?"

An apologetic look crossed Mr. Leery's face. "He must have forgotten, Joey. He went down to the station early with his mom to use some of the editing equipment there. You know, for that piece he's doing about the Australian girl."

Joey nodded. What a morning this was turning out to be! Dawson had made her get up early and haul her butt over, and then he had blown her off. He hadn't even had the courtesy to call her to cancel.

To top it all off, he was with that Australian girl again. Even if Joey and Dawson did get together, he'd probably moon about Sheila the whole time, like he did at the beach the other day.

"Thanks, Mr. Leery," Joey said quietly.

"I'm heading out now, but when I come back, I'll tell him that he's a scatterbrain," Mr. Leery called. "Don't worry."

"Scatterbrain" was a polite way of putting it, Joey thought, as she climbed out the window and down the ladder. What a jerk Dawson was! How could she have chosen him in that dream? *Nightmare*, she corrected. If she ever found herself in that situation in real life, she would be sure not only to choose Jeremy but to run Dawson down with the plane.

Joey stared out over the creek, toward her house. Well, she certainly couldn't go home right now. Bess was sure to rip her head off. Maybe she'd just dangle her feet off the dock for a while, till she was sure that her sister was gone, off somewhere playing family with Bodie and Alexander.

She pulled off her sneakers and socks and dangled her feet in the water. She leaned back, letting the morning sun beat down on her face. She tried to wipe her mind clean of everything: Jeremy, Dawson, Bess, life in general.

Her meditation was interrupted by Howard. Joey pulled out the key chain and checked the virtual pet. The pink egg suddenly made her sad. She remembered the day on the beach when she and Jeremy met, when he gently showed her how to clean up after Howard.

She didn't want to think about Jeremy anymore. It made her too sad, too angry. She took the egg and threw it into the creek. "Good-bye," she said bitterly. "I'll call. I'll be in touch. Yeah, right."

She pulled on her sneakers and socks. She thought about what she'd do all day. Maybe she'd just ride around town all day long.

She walked over to her bike. As soon as she mounted it, her conscience pulled her off. She saw a vision of Clarissa Cummings's sweet face turning sad when Joey gave her the news that Howard was gone. She also envisioned Jeremy, dressed like Victor Laszlo in *Casablanca*, disappearing into the fog. Finally, she pictured Bess, dark circles under her eyes, feeding the baby. Bess couldn't throw Alexander away when he was too much trouble, and Alex-

ander was much harder to care for than a virtual
pet.

What had she been thinking? Joey couldn't leave
Howard in the creek.

Rats! she thought. She couldn't do this to Clarissa. And she didn't want to throw away the memory of Jeremy, either. And maybe her sister really
did need her, she realized as she whipped off her
shoes and socks. She couldn't turn her back on her
own family, no matter how frighteningly screwed up
they were.

She had to find Howard. She hoped he was still
alive.

Joey ran back out onto the dock and dived into
the creek.

Pacey woke early on Monday and hurried to the
specialty coffee shop. "Two lattes," he told the guy
behind the register. He drummed his fingers on the
counter impatiently as the server grappled with the
milk-steaming machine. Pacey didn't want to be
late. He wanted to catch Jen before she left for lifesaving class.

He'd apologize to her and then take off. He certainly wasn't going to show his face in class anymore. It had been a joke for him to think he could
actually be a lifeguard, anyway. Somehow he didn't
fit the mold of the macho, heroic, babe-magnet rescue type.

Tim would get the hint that he wasn't coming
back. Pacey doubted that Tim or anyone else would
miss him anyway. Pacey certainly wouldn't miss the

lectures, but he was going to miss the morning routine.

That didn't matter, he realized. Jen probably wanted nothing to do with him. But he had to try to make amends anyway. He owed it to her. He owed it to himself.

After what seemed like an eternity, Pacey was served his two coffees. He quickly paid and raced out the door.

He arrived at Jen's house just as she was walking out the door. Pacey caught her by surprise. "Good morning," he said awkwardly.

At first Pacey thought Jen might grab the hot coffee from his hand and dump it over his head. He would deserve it, he thought.

But instead, she answered him pleasantly. "Morning, Pacey," she said.

Pacey handed her the latte. "Peace offering," he said.

Jen accepted it, pulled the lid off, and sat down on the porch steps. "I haven't been able to function correctly without it," she said, taking a swallow.

Pacey sat down next to her and took a sip of his coffee. "Listen, I want to apologize," he said. "I've been acting like a mega-idiot this past week."

Jen was silent for a few seconds. Pacey uncomfortably turned away and spotted Joey climbing down Dawson's ladder in a huff. He waved, but she didn't see him. Joey looked like she was in her own world.

"It's okay," Jen said softly, drawing Pacey's attention away from Joey.

Pacey shook his head. He took another sip of

coffee and swallowed. "It's not okay," he said. "I was rude to you. And you were only trying to help— trying to be my friend. I don't know what gets into me sometimes. Now that I've been humiliated in class, I can say good-bye to any hope of starting over."

"That's not true," Jen said. "All you have to do is be yourself."

Pacey shook his head and sighed. "That won't work either. Girls my own age just don't find anything remotely attractive about me."

Jen put her coffee down and gave Pacey a tender look. "That's not true," she said.

Pacey knew Jen was just trying to be nice. "Nah," he said. "Unfortunately you are wrong."

"I'm right," Jen said. "I know a girl your age who does find you attractive. I know a girl your age who sees many things to like about you."

Pacey looked at Jen as if he thought she was crazy. "Like who?" he asked doubtfully.

"Like me," Jen said. "I think you're cute and sweet, and you have a great sense of humor." She laughed. "That is, when you're acting like the real you—not your evil twin. The real you is a catch."

Pacey couldn't believe what he was hearing.

Jen went on. "And maybe I was a little jealous the other day. Maybe I was developing the slightest bit of a crush on you."

For a moment Pacey didn't know what to say. But then his eyes widened. "So I was right? You want me! You have the hots for me!"

"I said a tiny crush," Jen said. "Before your ego blows up again, the key word there was 'was.' I liked the friendship we were developing. I want to keep it that way, okay?"

Pacey nodded. She was right. They were really just starting to get to know each other well. He wanted to have a friendship with Jen before he started ruining things.

"I think someday you're going to find a very lucky girl, a girl you can feel comfortable around—so comfortable that you can just be yourself," Jen added.

Now Pacey was getting embarrassed. He looked at his watch. "Hey, you're going to be late for class."

"Me?" Jen asked. "You mean 'we.'"

"No," Pacey said, shaking his head. "You. I've decided I'm not cut out to save lives. I'm better off shelving videotapes."

Jen looked disappointed. "You shouldn't give up, Pacey. You can do this if you'll just pay attention in class and take it seriously." She stopped and raised her eyebrows. "I can tutor you on the stuff you missed."

Pacey nodded. That didn't sound like such a bad proposition. "Okay," he said, standing up, "but only if you promise not to spit in my face when you lecture."

Jen giggled. "Deal," she said. She stuck out her hand. "Friends, though, okay?"

But before Pacey could shake it, they heard a loud splash and turned toward the creek.

Why in the world was Joey going for a swim so early in the morning?

"What's with her?" Pacey said. "She just plunged into the creek fully clothed."

Jen squinted curiously at Joey in the creek. Pacey could see Joey's head bob in and out of the water a few times. She almost seemed to be diving for something.

"What is she doing?" Jen asked.

"It's hard to tell with her," Pacey said. "She's been acting so weird lately, like in a good mood—" Pacey stopped.

He turned toward Jen. "Where is she?" he asked. "Did you see her come up that time?"

"No," Jen said.

Without another word, Pacey and Jen raced to the creek.

Dawson came in the front door. The house was quiet. No one was home.

He was so mad at himself. He'd forgotten one of the tapes he needed, and he didn't have much time left to use the equipment at the station before the editing crew got in.

He ran up the stairs and into his room. He had accomplished a lot this morning, however. When he finished the tape, Sheila was definitely going to be wowed. He'd call her and ask if he could bring by a surprise for her. He hoped she would say yes and they'd be friends again.

He rifled through his video rack and picked out the tape he'd forgotten. He perked up when he heard a commotion outside.

He moved to the window and saw Jen and Pacey dash toward the creek, shouting something. They must be practicing some lifesaving technique, he figured, but why were they yelling so loud and why so early in the morning?

He picked up his camera and zoomed out the window for a close-up. This way, he could really see what was going on.

He saw Jen, then Pacey, dive into the creek.

What in the world were they doing? They didn't seem to be practicing. They seemed anxious and panicked.

That's when he spotted it.

The bike.

Joey's bike.

He slapped himself on the forehead. He'd forgotten all about her! They were supposed to go biking this morning! How could he have been such an idiot?

Joey was probably furious. She'd never forgive him now. He wouldn't blame her if she didn't.

Wait—if Joey's bike was here, then where was Joey?

He got his answer when he saw Pacey pull her limp body out of the water, while Jen helped him lift her onto the dock.

Chapter 19

Pacey had hit the water right next to Jen. He had spotted Joey right away. She was unconscious. Jen figured she must have hit her head on Dawson's rowboat while surfacing.

"I got her," Pacey yelled as he towed Joey through the water. Jen reached them and helped lift Joey onto the dock. They laid her out flat.

Quickly Jen checked Joey's pulse while she mentally reviewed her CPR lessons.

"Is she breathing?" Pacey asked urgently.

"No," Jen said. Instantly she started to give her artificial respiration. Jen carefully tilted Joey's head back. Then, while holding her nose closed, she breathed into Joey's mouth.

She waited a few seconds, then repeated the procedure. She waited again, then repeated it once more.

Pacey watched. Jen could feel his nervous energy, but she knew she had to stay cool.

Jen repeated the respiration one last time.

"You can do it," Pacey encouraged. "You know what you're doing. Everything's going to be okay."

Finally Joey came to, coughing up water.

When Joey regained consciousness, she didn't know what was happening. All she did know was that Jen Lindley was cradling her, asking if she was all right, and Pacey was standing above her, staring at her as if he had seen a ghost.

Joey searched her memory for what had happened. She remembered diving into the creek. She remembered searching around for Howard. She remembered finally spotting him, retrieving him, and shoving him into her pocket while she was underwater.

Then she didn't remember anything else. But her head sure hurt.

"Are you okay," Jen asked again.

Joey realized she should answer or Jen would think she was brain-damaged. She sat up, wobbly. "I'm fine. I must have hit my head." As she looked at Jen, something occurred to her. "Did you—did you save my life?"

Jen didn't say anything.

But Pacey said, "Yes, she did, and, boy, are you ever lucky that the best lifesaver in the class was around. Jen had the situation totally under control. She knew exactly what to do."

Jen smiled at Pacey. "Pacey pulled you out of the creek."

Pacey ducked his head. For once he had no wisecrack ready. He grinned at Joey.

Joey regarded Jen and Pacey with awe, then embarrassment. "Thanks," she said. "I don't know what to say. Thank you so much."

"We should get you to a hospital to get your head checked out," Jen said. "Make sure you don't have a concussion."

"Okay," Joey said. "But I just need to sit here for a few seconds." She felt worn out, freaked out, and a little dizzy. This sure was weird.

And to make things even weirder, Dawson suddenly ran out of his house, camera in hand. When he got close to Joey, he tossed the camera aside, pushed Jen and Pacey out of the way, and took Joey in his arms.

"Are you okay?" Dawson said in a panic. "I—I'm sorry I forgot about this morning!" He seemed to be on the verge of tears. "I promise I'll never forget about you again. Ever."

Then an even weirder thing happened.

Out of nowhere, Dawson planted a huge wet kiss right on her lips. A warm, lingering, kiss.

When he pulled away, Joey looked at him in shock. Those feelings skittered through her all over again. Her expression then slowly changed from shock to tenderness.

"Don't ever leave me," Dawson said.

Joey giggled, thinking about Dawson in his Humphrey Bogart garb. "I won't," she answered.

And suddenly, though she had been daydreaming about leaving Capeside behind, right then and there, with her friends around her, Joey never wanted to leave. She never wanted to have any best friend except Dawson Leery. And she certainly wanted to stick around to kiss him again.

And she didn't want to leave her family—Bess, Bodie, and Alexander. Though they were as ragtag as a family could get, they were all she had. Joey didn't want to lose them ever.

She vowed to do her best, from then on, to help them stay a family. Forever.

When Pacey and Jen showed up late for class that day, Tim was not pleased. They and Dawson had taken Joey to the hospital. She was examined and released right away, since she had no injuries beyond the bump on her head, but Pacey and Jen didn't get to class until nearly lunchtime.

Tim stopped lecturing. "How nice of you two to show up!" he growled. "Ms. Lindley, I'm surprised at you. Don't tell me you spent the morning goofing off with Witter?"

"Quite the opposite," Pacey answered. "We actually spent the morning saving a friend from drowning."

Tim's eyes narrowed in a threatening squint. "I'm sick and tired of your excuses and your lame attempts at humor, Witter." Tim stared Pacey down, then turned to Jen. "I'll get a real answer from Ms. Lindley. Why are you two late?"

"Pacey is telling the truth," she said. "We had to pull a friend out of the creek this morning and take her to the hospital."

The class gasped and whispered and mumbled. Tim blew his whistle. Pacey was sure that he didn't believe them. "Tell us what happened," Tim said calmly.

As Pacey and Jen related the story, Pacey enjoyed the looks of awe and wonder he was getting from his classmates, both male and female. But he wasn't going to take the credit. He pointed out that Jen was the one who had really saved Joey's life.

But then Jen added that Pacey was the one who was alert and watching. He had noticed the swimmer in distress, and he had pulled Joey out of the creek. That made Pacey feel great. For once, he had done something right.

"You did the right things, though it was dangerous, as you are novice lifesavers," Tim said when they had finished. He smiled, then, for the first time ever in class. Pacey nearly winced at how unnatural a smile looked on his usually expressionless face. "I'm proud of you," he said. "Both of you."

Then class resumed as usual, and Pacey and Jen took their seats and listened to the lecture. This time, Pacey was attentive. Even if he never became a lifeguard, he wanted to know how to save lives. He was in awe of how capable Jen was and how she took calm control of the whole situation.

And even though Pacey knew he'd probably end up working at Screenplay Video again, wearing a dumb black vest, he would have skills that he could use for the rest of his life. Skills that could save a friend. Skills that could save a child. Or even, skills that could save a bikini-clad damsel in distress.

When Joey walked into the house with a bandage on her head that afternoon, Bess ran over to her. "What happened?" she asked, concerned.

Joey sat down and told Bess the whole story. She

told her how Pacey and Jen had saved her life. She told her about Dawson's kiss. And as she talked, she realized that she hadn't had a real conversation with her sister in days.

She then filled Bess in on the events of the past few days. She described her day at the beach and her last night with Jeremy. She told her about how he played the saxophone in the restaurant and dedicated the song to her. Bess's face grew sad when she told her it was one of Mom's favorite songs. Then they shared a laugh over her weird *Casablanca* dream, and they laughed even more about Howard, who was miraculously still alive after the whole ordeal.

"We're going to have to have a special celebration at the Icehouse tonight," Bess said. "I want to thank your friends for saving the life of my only sister." Her eyes grew a little watery. "I don't know what I'd do without you, kid," she whispered.

"Thanks, Bess," Joey said. "You can count on me from now on. I realize that I've been acting like a selfish brat lately."

When the baby started to cry, Joey was the first to move. "I'll change him," she offered.

"Thanks for the offer," Bess said, "but today I want you to rest up. Tomorrow, on the other hand," she said with a grin, "he's all yours."

As Bess changed Alexander, her face lit up. "Oh! I almost forgot to tell you! There's a message on the machine for you."

Joey pressed the play button on the answering machine. A familiar voice came out of the speaker: "Hi, Joey. This is Jeremy. We just stopped for a bite to eat on the road, and I wanted to call you and let you know that I haven't stopped thinking about you the whole time. I'll call you when I get home. I miss you. Bye."

Joey smiled, a warm feeling spreading from her heart all throughout her body as she looked back on the whirlwind week she'd just had. It felt good to have two men in her life: one her soul mate and friend for life; the other a mysterious romantic stranger who could appear at any time, stir things up, and make life interesting.

Life could be a lot worse, she thought.

Chapter 20

Dawson was shaken up all day after Joey nearly drowned. At Screenplay, he could barely concentrate. He just stared into space, but it didn't matter much, because he had only a few customers.

He did have one surprise customer, however. Sheila stopped by—without the babies.

"Where are your other two-thirds?" Dawson asked.

Sheila laughed lightly. "The Barclays are back from their trip. They've given me some time off," she explained. "It feels great."

There was an awkward pause, but Sheila broke it first. "I wanted to apologize for the way I reacted the other day. I didn't mean to be so harsh," she said. "It's just that . . . I can't really explain it." She paused.

Dawson stepped in. "Listen, I think I understand.

But I have a surprise for you," he said. "Can you come by my house tonight?"

"Okay," Sheila agreed. "What time?"

"I work until six," Dawson explained. "How about seven or so?"

"Sounds good," Sheila said. Then she smiled her dazzling smile, dimples lighting up her whole face. She gave Dawson a small wave and left.

Dawson was glad he would have an opportunity to fix things with Sheila. Though he'd decided that his heart belonged to Joey, he wanted to stay friends with Sheila. He was happy that she'd stopped by. He couldn't wait to show her the tape tonight.

When the doorbell rang at precisely seven o'clock, Dawson had everything ready. The tape was cued up, and he had even chosen some great music to go with his glowing piece on Sheila.

Mr. Leery answered the door. Dawson had instructed his parents not to say a word to Sheila. When his mom gave him a curious look, Dawson told her that the tape was a surprise.

Dawson came down to greet Sheila and he led her up to his room. He threw open the door with a grand gesture. "This is where it all happens," he said.

Sheila laughed when she saw all of the movie posters on the walls. "Just what I expected," she said. She picked up Dawson's E.T. doll. "I love E.T.!" she exclaimed. "I always wanted one. . . ." Her voice trailed off. She changed the subject and placed the doll back on Dawson's bed. "So what is the grand surprise?"

Dawson patted the edge of his bed. "Have a seat," he said, then shut off all the lights and pressed Play.

Sheila came on the screen. A voice-over described "a spunky young Australian who came to the U.S. and works as a nanny to newborn twins." A montage followed, with Sheila feeding, changing, and playing with the twins.

But while Dawson beamed at his work, Sheila looked as if she might cry. And eventually she did. She burst into tears and grabbed the remote off Dawson's bed. While Dawson flicked on the lights, she stopped the tape.

"What's wrong?" Dawson asked, rushing to her side. He put an arm around her.

Sheila pulled away. "You can't put this on the news," she said through her tears. "You simply can't. I beg you."

Dawson leaned closer to Sheila curiously. "Of course I won't if you don't want me to. I—I just thought that if you could see how great you looked, you'd change your mind. I know you said you were shy, but I guess I just didn't understand. I'm sorry."

Sheila took a deep breath and stopped crying. "I'm not shy, Dawson. I know you meant well." She took another deep breath. "I'll tell you the truth, because I trust you. Then you'll understand, and you'll see why you can't show this.

"I left Australia when I was seventeen. My parents had split up. My father disappeared. My mother took up with an awful man." She paused for breath. "So I left. I wanted to start over as far away as possible. I packed up everything I owned and came to Providence.

"I lied about Boston," she went on. "I never went there. Providence seemed just perfect—big enough to be anonymous, but cheap enough to live, and small enough so as not to be overwhelming."

Dawson hugged Sheila encouragingly. She went on. "When you're seventeen and a foreigner, and you haven't finished school, it's hard to find decent work to support yourself. I did find a job in a clothing store. . . ." Her voice faltered. "But I had a hard time making ends meet. Then I got into some trouble. I fell in with another girl who was stealing from the store and selling the clothes. The store owners didn't press charges, and the police let me go."

She stopped again. "So I scoured the newspapers, and I answered an ad for a live-in nanny."

"It's okay," Dawson consoled her. "It's okay."

She went on. "I figured the nanny job was perfect, because I love kids, I would have a roof over my head, and the money was good. I had a lot of babysitting experience in Australia—I was always taking care of the neighbors' kids. Though I didn't have any other credentials, I gave the Barclays my old neighbors' numbers. They had no idea I had run away. My mother doesn't live anywhere near there now. She probably doesn't even care."

She stopped short and started to cry again. Dawson hushed her and cradled her in his arms.

After a few minutes she composed herself and went on. "So you see," she continued, "if someone in Providence were to see your news story and tell the Barclays about my past, I would lose everything.

They are wonderful, loving people. Please, Dawson, I don't want to lose my job. And my home."

Dawson was stunned. It must have been rough for Sheila, running away at such a young age. And when she finally found her niche, Dawson had almost ruined her life. He couldn't believe how thoughtless he had been. He should have just let it go when she initially said no. "I don't know what to say," he said, "except that I'm really, really sorry."

But actions spoke louder than words, Dawson figured. He got up, took the tape from the VCR, and unspooled it, destroying it right before her eyes. "Your secret is safe with me. I'll destroy all the other tapes I have, too."

"Thank you, Dawson," Sheila said, a few last tears streaming down her face.

Dawson took a tissue from his night table and dabbed at her eyes. "You can trust me," Dawson assured her.

"I know," Sheila whispered. "I know I can."

By the time Dawson walked Sheila home, she had composed herself. She told Dawson she felt a lot better, and Dawson apologized again for everything.

He gave her a kiss on the cheek, and once again assured her that he would never again do anything to jeopardize her security.

As he walked back home through the cool summer afternoon, the breeze from the creek washed over him. He remembered the first night he'd spotted Sheila. He remembered wishing for an exciting summer.

If this first week was any indication, the summer would be full of twists and turns and surprises.

When he walked into the house, Dawson's mother said eagerly, "When do I get my story?"

"I'm sorry, Mom, I couldn't get Sheila's permission," Dawson explained. "I'm afraid that she's painfully camera-shy."

Mrs. Leery's face fell. "Oh, Dawson," she said, her voice full of disappointment, "I was looking forward to that piece!" She paused, thoughtfully. "But if we can't get her permission, then we're up against a legal wall."

"Don't worry, Mom," Dawson assured her with a jubilant grin. "I have an even better story for you. How about 'Teens Training as Lifeguards Save a Drowning Girl'—right on Leery property?"

"Is that for real?" his Mom asked, her eyes widening.

"I've got the exclusive," Dawson assured her. "Film at eleven."

Bess and Bodie opened the Icehouse that night for a special occasion: the celebration of Joey's rescue. Joey, Jen, Dawson, and Pacey sat around a wooden table, the whole restaurant to themselves. Bess came to take their orders.

"Everything's free," she said, giving Joey a quick hug. "For saving my baby sister's life."

Pacey and Dawson locked eyes. "In that case, we're going to chow down," Pacey said excitedly.

"Anything you want," Bess assured them, as Bodie came by with a full bottle of sparkling apple cider and six glasses.

"Heads up!" Bodie said, as he unscrewed the cap. Joey and Jen took cover from the foam that escaped from the bottle. He carefully poured a glass for each person.

"A toast!" Bess announced. "To heroic acts!"

They lifted their glasses, clinking them happily.

"I have a toast," Joey said between sips. "To family and friends," she said. "You guys are the best."

Pacey clanged his fork on his glass. "One more," he said. "To Jen's television debut and mine, courtesy of director extraordinaire Dawson Leery."

They all raised their glasses again. "I'm not finished yet," Pacey said. "And to Jen, who taught me to try to be myself, because my alter ego is even worse than I am."

They all laughed, but they grew quiet as dusk began to fall and the sunset threw an orange glow over the restaurant. It was a magical summer night, Joey thought. A summer night you could have only in Capeside.

About the Creator/Executive Producer

Born in New Bern, North Carolina, Kevin Williamson studied theater and film at East Carolina University before moving to New York to pursue an acting career. He relocated to Los Angeles and took a job as an assistant to a music video director. Eventually deciding to explore his gift for storytelling, Williamson took an extension course in screenwriting at UCLA (University of California, Los Angeles).

Kevin Williamson has experienced incredible success in the film medium. His first feature film was *Scream*, directed by Wes Craven and starring Drew Barrymore, Courteney Cox and Neve Campbell. He has also written other feature films including the psychological thriller *I Know What You Did Last Summer*, based on the Lois Duncan novel, and directed by Jim Gillespie. His first foray into television, *Dawson's Creek™*, has already received high praise from television critics for its honest portrayal of teen life.

About the Author

K. S. Rodriguez is an entertainment glutton who
has written several books about television and
movie personalities. She lives in New York City
amid a clutter of magazines, newspapers, videos,
and CDs with her husband, Ronnie.